FAR FROM FAIR

FAR FROM FAIR

Elana K. Arnold

HOUGHTON MIFFLIN HARCOURT | BOSTON NEW YORK

The text was set in Charter ITC Std.
Hand-lettering and art by Julie McLaughlin
Design by Sharismar Rodriguez

Library of Congress Cataloging-in-Publication Data is available.
ISBN 978-0-544-60227-4

Manufactured in the United States of America
DOC 10 9 8 7 6 5 4 3 2 1
4500577852

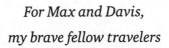

For Max and Davis,
my brave fellow travelers

The Ugliest Thing

I T WAS THE ugliest thing she had ever seen. Obnoxiously ugly. Embarrassingly ugly. Epically ugly. And it was sitting in her family's driveway.

Actually, no. It was sitting in the Waldmans' driveway—or, at least, what would shortly become the Waldmans' driveway when escrow closed in a few days and the house Odette Zyskowski grew up in wouldn't be her home anymore. That *thing* would be her home. That run-down, beat-up brown-and-brown RV that Mom and Dad had just pulled up in, honking what was intended to be a cheerful beep, but instead sounded like the mournful death cry of a desperate whale.

Odette looked behind herself at the house, trying to ignore the SOLD banner splashed across the FOR SALE sign stuck in the front lawn. She had never given the house much thought. It was just a house. But now she saw the brick path winding through the grass from the sidewalk, uneven and tipsy, and it occurred to Odette that she knew every brick on that path—which ones were chipped, which listed slightly to the side, which were stamped with the bricklayer's name, Steinberg & Sons.

She saw the bright red front door, the door she slammed through every afternoon at 3:14 p.m. Behind that door, Odette knew, was the mud bench where she ditched her backpack and shoes. She saw the wide, bright windows, the shutters that framed them. She took in the dark shingle roof that her parents had been talking about replacing for years but would soon become the Waldmans' problem.

It was a beautiful home.

Mom cut the engine of the RV, and Dad threw open the metal door on the side and a set of two steps popped out.

Rex stood next to Odette, rocking up onto the balls of his feet, the way he did when he got excited. "Awesome, awesome, awesome," he chanted to himself, and when Dad called, "So, what do you guys think?" Rex shouted "Awesome!" and ran full speed into Dad, butting his head into Dad's stomach and grinding it against him.

Dad said "Oof!" and laughed, and Mom, coming out of the RV, said, "Careful, buddy," and then she asked Odette, "So, honey, what do you think?" but Odette was already heading back into the Waldmans' house, slamming the red door shut behind her.

Hands

ODETTE'S ROOM WAS at the end of the hall, just before the turn to her parents' bedroom. The hall was stacked with boxes, piled three high and labeled in thick black Sharpie ink: REX'S ROOM (STORAGE); LINENS AND BEDDING (STORAGE); BATHROOM MISC. (YARD SALE); BOOKS (LIBRARY GIVEAWAY); BATHROOM ESSENTIALS (COACH).

That was what Mom was calling the RV: the "Coach." The word brought a few things to Odette's mind—baseball, for one, a sport she found endlessly boring but still somehow comforting; Mr. Santiago, the track-and-field coach at Odette's middle school, who after he'd seen her run the mile in PE had spent most of Odette's sixth grade year trying to recruit her to the team; and Cinderella's pumpkin-turned-coach that she took to the ball.

None of these images had anything to do with Mom's

use of the word in sentences like "When we pick up the Coach, the first thing we'll do is fix up your private space, Detters" (which was what she liked to call Odette), and "It might not look like much in the pictures, kids, but the Coach has under twenty thousand miles on it and is as snug as a bug inside."

The Coach. Sitting in the driveway. Odette couldn't get far enough away, no matter how good a runner she was. So she had to content herself with slamming her bedroom door—hard enough to make the windows rattle—and throwing herself face-down onto the bed.

Her sheets smelled like home. The same detergent her mom had been using as long as Odette had been aware of detergent smell. Probably before that. And even with her eyes closed and her face pressed into her bedspread, Odette could perfectly picture her room. The pale blue walls. The light pink ceiling, a gently whirling fan just above her bed. The windows, looking out over the back-yard, with their gossamer-thin ballooning white curtains.

And more: the seven pillows she arranged each morning after making her bed, and then restacked each night on the carpet before climbing between her sheets. Two yellow, one pink, one green, two blue, one red.

There wouldn't be room for her seven throw pillows in the Coach. "You can bring one," Mom had told her.

One. Absolutely ridiculous.

When the knock came at her door, Odette ignored it. She knew it was Dad from the way he knocked—always a little pattern, a little song, not just straight across with all his knuckles.

She heard him open the door anyway, even though she hadn't said "Come in," and that bothered her too, that lack of respect, that lack of privacy, and the mean little voice in her head taunted, *You'd better get used to it, Odette. There won't be much privacy in the Coach.*

Her dad cleared his throat. Odette could tell that he was still lurking just inside the doorway. That was her dad—a lurker. He was always ho-ing and hum-ing about decisions, weighing the costs and benefits. Mom sometimes said, "You're going to drive me crazy, Simon! Just *do* something!"

But he didn't usually do *anything*—at least, not anything important. He'd ho and hum until Odette's mom got tired of waiting and just did it herself—whatever it was that needed doing. Choosing which car to buy. Picking the toppings for the pizza.

And then, three months ago, Odette's dad had *done something*. Something big. Something crazy.

"They were going to lay off three guys," she heard Dad telling Mom. "Three guys who actually *like* their jobs. And with Sissy being so sick, not to mention the trouble we've been having with us . . . with each other . . . I thought, well, I guess I thought it couldn't make things any worse."

It was late at night, and Dad hadn't gotten home from the office in time for dinner, which wasn't that unusual. Odette was supposed to be asleep, like Rex was in his room (dark blue with deep-sea ocean fish painted on the walls and a jellyfish diorama on his bookcase), but she wasn't. She was sneaking out to the kitchen for a cookie. And there were her parents, sitting at the table, with only the small sink light turned on. They were holding hands.

It looked so strange, their hands. Fingers interwoven, like the kids at school, like they were announcing to the world that they were a couple. It wasn't something Odette was used to seeing between her parents. Usually, if anyone was holding anyone's hand, it was Mom and Rex. Sometimes Dad and Rex. But never Mom and Dad.

Odette had backed slowly down the hall toward her room. What did that mean, to lay someone off? And what did Dad mean, that whatever he had done couldn't make things any worse?

Odette knew Grandma Sissy wasn't healthy. Not that Mom and Dad had told her all the details, but Odette knew. She'd heard Mom on the phone with Grandma Sissy, asking about doctor appointments and pain medication and nausea. But that other thing that Dad had said, about trouble between him and Mom . . . Odette didn't know what to think about that.

When she woke up the next morning, she had forgotten all about the night before, the table, the handholding. And she walked into the kitchen ready to find what she always found: Rex expounding about something that fascinated him—queer ocean life, or rare types of pygmy animals that were legal to own as pets, or the best way to make applesauce—and her mother nodding and pretending to listen while making their breakfast and packing their lunches.

Instead she found them—her parents—sitting again at the table, holding hands. Holding hands, again. For a minute she thought they hadn't moved, but then she saw that Mom was dressed, not in her robe, and that Dad was wearing his weekend clothes instead of the rumpled suit he'd been in last night, even though this was a Thursday. And Rex was with them, eating oatmeal and whacking his feet against the bottom of the table in a rhythmic thumping beat that sounded to Odette the way a zombie might sound dragging a non-working leg behind himself.

And then Dad had smiled — something else she hadn't seen much of lately, come to think of it, and Mom said, "Good morning, Detters," and then they proceeded to ruin her life.

Not Okay

"YOU WANT TO talk, Odette?" asked Dad.

She shook her head into the bedspread, still refusing to look up.

He sighed. Odette imagined him shifting his weight, leaning against her door frame.

"No," she said into the mattress.

There was a pause. Then he said, "It's going to be okay, honey. I promise." More lurking, and then Odette heard him walk away. He left the door open.

Odette sighed and flipped onto her back. She was beginning to feel smothered, face-down on her bed. The house was hot.

The Coach has air conditioning! Odette could imagine Mom's peppy response.

Dad promised it would be okay. He *promised.* As if

he had that kind of authority. That kind of pull with the universe. Odette knew a lie when she heard one. How on earth could he know everything would be okay? To Odette, it was clear as a glass of water that things were *not* okay. Not by a mile.

The Jamboree

"THEY BROUGHT IT home last night," Odette told Mieko the next day at school. It was the last period of the day—PE—and today they had to run the mile one last time. All sixth-graders had to run the mile three times, once at the beginning of the school year, once in the middle, and once more at the end. Most kids complained about it, and a few even tried playing sick, but Coach Santiago made them make it up the next day.

Odette and Mieko were stretching with the rest of the class. They were on the lawn in the center of the track, which wound around them like a wide, flat ribbon. Odette liked running, and so did Mieko, so neither of them was complaining, but some of the kids were trying to devise last-minute escape plans, spending their energy freaking out instead of conserving it for the run.

"The Coach?" asked Mieko. She'd spent lots of afternoons at Odette's place. She'd heard Odette's mom and dad comparing the various secondhand RVs they'd been checking out and had looked over their shoulders at the pictures on the computer screen. "Did they pick the Weekender?"

Odette shook her head. "The Jamboree."

"Ooh," said Mieko. "Tough blow."

Coach Santiago blew his whistle then, and Odette was glad, because running would be better than talking about the Coach, and the SOLD sign, and the boxes lining the hallway, Mom's daily calls with Grandma Sissy, the pinched, worried look on her face each time she hung up, and the annoying high-pitched whistling Dad had been doing since he took the "voluntary layoff" and the severance package at his job.

They lined up in groups of five, alphabetically. Coach Santiago held his whistle between his teeth, his stopwatch in his hand, and noted the start time for each group of runners. Mieko was in one of the middle groups (Ishida), but Odette had to wait until the very last whistle before she could spring off the pads of her feet and let go, before she could let the breaths grow sharp in her lungs and relax into the pace of her strides.

Before she could fly.

The Long Blue Tunnel

ONCE, THREE YEARS ago when Odette was nine and Rex was just five, back when he was still having furies almost every day, Grandma Sissy had come for a visit. It was longer than a regular visit because Dad had been out of town on business.

Dad had called every night. He said the same things—*I miss you, I love you, I'll be home soon*—but he wouldn't say when, precisely.

"The best way out is always through," Odette heard Grandma Sissy tell Rex at the playground when he hesitated at the mouth of the play structure's long blue tunnel.

"The best way out is always through," Odette heard Grandma Sissy tell Mom at the kitchen table, where she sat with puffy eyes and a pursed-tight mouth.

One day two weeks into the visit, Grandma Sissy took

Odette to the grocery store to buy sugar. Odette was carrying the three-pound pink and white sack to the counter when she saw someone who looked just like Dad paying the cashier for a small bag of groceries, two Hungry Man frozen dinners at the very top.

"That looks like Dad," Odette said to Grandma Sissy, and in the very same breath she realized that it *was* her dad.

"Dad!" Odette raised one hand to wave, and the bag of sugar slipped from her other hand and exploded at her feet, a wave of cool white crystals burying her toes. She slip-slid through the sugar and ran to him, but when she got up close she saw that his shirt was crumpled and his eyes were filled with tears, and she wondered, for a second, if she was wrong after all, if this wasn't her dad but just someone who looked like him.

Then he smiled, and said, "Honey," and reached out his arms.

Odette had ridden home from the store in Dad's car, his Hungry Man dinners in the back seat, Grandma Sissy following behind.

At nine years old, Odette had thought it was weird

that Dad would have gone to the grocery store instead of heading straight home from his business trip. But at twelve and a half, as she rounded the last turn—first in her group—and blazed past Coach Santiago and his stopwatch, her thighs fire-tight, her chest gripped by iron, she remembered that day all in a rush and she saw, suddenly, that her dad hadn't left town at all.

No Music

"MOM AND DAD are dancing in the dining room," Rex told Odette.

He was interrupting her, which he knew he wasn't supposed to do, so Odette ignored him, pretending that she hadn't heard, keeping her eyes tight on the screen of her phone, thumbing through the pictures the kids at school were posting of the last few days of the year: the quad brim-full during the final assembly; Principal Williams yelling something into a megaphone.

Rex didn't go away. "They're *slow* dancing," he said. "Like people do in movies."

Odette abandoned the pretense of disinterest and stood up from the couch. Rex led the way, bouncing up onto the balls of his feet with each step.

Rex never lied. Never. So they must be dancing. But, still, seeing them there—*slow dancing*—Mom's arms around Dad's neck, her head resting on his chest, Dad's chin on her head, his arms around her waist, was not only surprising but also . . . weird. For one thing, there wasn't even any music on.

"See?" Rex whispered.

"Yeah," Odette answered. "Come on." She tugged on his arm, pulling him away from the doorway.

"They're really bad dancers," Rex said, in the kitchen.

Odette pulled out a box of macaroni and cheese. "Are you hungry?"

Rex shrugged. "I could eat."

Zombie Caesar

THEIR FRONT YARD looked like a furniture store. Dad had moved the Coach around the corner to make room for the yard sale traffic, and a steady stream of cars and pickup trucks had been pulling up to the curb since six o'clock in the morning, a full hour before the yard sale was supposed to start.

"If you build it, they will come," Dad said, standing in the driveway between their L-shaped leather sofa, the one they curled up onto each week for Friday movie night, and the matched set of wingback chairs from the formal living room that no one ever sat in.

It was a line from some old baseball movie, and Odette became instantly angry when Dad said it. Today wasn't about *building*—it was about destroying.

"Would you take two dollars for this?" asked a lady

with a ridiculously high ponytail. She was holding a blue glass vase that was clearly marked *five* dollars.

"No way," said Odette. "Five dollars."

The woman put the vase down on a table full of knick-knacks.

Triumph surged through Odette, as if she'd just won a small but important victory.

"We're trying to get rid of things, not scare away the customers," said Mom.

Odette shrugged. "That thing is worth way more than five dollars."

"There's no room for it in the Coach," said Mom. "It's worth whatever someone is willing to pay for it."

Odette wanted to say something mean—she hadn't quite found the words, but she knew exactly the tone she wanted to use—but then Rex came barreling out of the house with another box of his toys and all of Mom's attention shifted immediately to him.

"Hey, buddy," said Mom. "What've you got there?"

"I wanna sell these, too," Rex said.

Odette could see that the box was full of Rex's miniature animal collection. Last year he'd been obsessed with Cubes—clear plastic boxes sold at the zoo gift store, each filled with a different collection of animals. Farm animals, dinosaurs, sea creatures, safari animals, on and on. Each Cube cost $15.95. Rex had wrangled a deal with Mom where she bought him a new one each month. She and Rex visited the local zoo together every fourth Saturday. It was their "special time," Mom called it.

"Are you sure, buddy? You've been collecting these for a while," Mom said.

"Yeah, I'm sure," said Rex. "I'm not really into them anymore. I want money. Lots of money."

Mom laughed and patted Rex's shoulder. "Okay," she said. "How much do you want for them?"

Odette turned away. She wasn't interested in hearing their pricing structure. There was Dad, helping an old guy load a table saw into the back of a truck. Odette hadn't even known that thing buried in the back of the garage *was* a table saw, so it wasn't like it was special or anything, but still Odette hated the old guy for buying it and found herself hoping that he'd cut through his finger the first time he used it.

She flopped into one of the wingback chairs. It was stiff and upright, not comfortable like their couch.

The day was beautiful. Big bright sky. Warm air. The

branches of the willow tree across the street bobbed and danced. Car after car pulled up to her house and left with her family's stuff.

Odette's phone vibrated in her pocket. A text from Mieko saying she was coming over. Odette couldn't muster the energy to text back.

With every knickknack, plate, piece of furniture, and book that got loaded into a stranger's car, Odette felt the reality of her situation deepen. Everything. She was losing everything.

Yesterday had been the last day of school. A big party, lockers being cleaned out, excited chatter and laughter all around her. Everyone was passing around yearbooks, writing stuff like *See you next year!* And *Let's hang out this summer!*

Odette had picked up her yearbook like everyone else. But she'd just shoved it in her backpack. Half the people would write stupid stuff about how much they'd miss her, when they didn't even know her. The other half would want to hear about where she was going and why she was leaving, which Odette didn't want to talk about. Which Odette didn't completely understand herself.

For Odette, it felt like a funeral. The end of everything.

That afternoon, when Odette was officially no longer a sixth-grader, Grandma Sissy had called to congratulate her on finishing the school year. "How's my adventurer?" Grandma Sissy asked. Her voice sounded like it always did, and Odette had wondered if maybe her parents were using Grandma Sissy's sickness as an excuse to make it okay that Dad was leaving his job and they were selling the house.

"I'm okay," Odette had lied. "How are you?"

"I've had better days, but I've had worse," Grandma Sissy said. "Tell me everything."

Odette didn't feel like talking, but she told Grandma Sissy about the yard sale plans, about the last day of school, about the Jamboree.

"Are you excited at all?" Grandma Sissy asked.

Odette shrugged, which she knew Grandma Sissy couldn't see through the telephone line. She didn't have words for the way she felt.

"Even in the bad," Grandma Sissy had said, and Odette recognized this as the beginning of one of Grandma Sissy's sayings, "there is opportunity for good. Odette, darling, you may feel powerless over what is happening to you right now—"

"Detters!" Mom called from where she was sorting clothes and blankets for the yard sale. "I need you to come keep an eye on your brother!"

"I've gotta go," Odette said, half glad to hang up. She didn't much feel like hearing Grandma Sissy's good advice.

But now, watching her family's stuff turn into other people's stuff, Odette wondered how Grandma Sissy had planned to end that sentence. *You may feel powerless over what is happening to you right now* ... What could she have said, after that? A conjunction, probably, followed by uplifting promises. *You may feel powerless over what is happening to you right now, but it will all turn out for the best.* Or, *but you'll see that things aren't really so bad.* Maybe, *but the future is full of surprises.*

After a while, Mieko appeared on her bike. She rode standing up, pedaling hard for a few strokes and then gliding, her back tall, her legs locked straight.

Odette would recognize Mieko even in shadow, from the way she rode her bike. She was both graceful and powerful, and she steered through the crowd of cars and bargain-hunters as if she were their queen.

"Hey." She hopped off her bike. She unclipped her helmet and hung it on the handlebar. "This is crazy!"

Odette nodded. Her cheeks and eyes felt heavy—her whole face did. Actually, her whole body, as if she were subjected to more gravity than the people around her. It felt maybe like zombification—numbing, slowing down, petrification.

Mieko flopped into the other wingback chair. "It's funny that we never sat in these when they were *inside* your house."

Odette nodded. Speech took too much energy.

Mieko pursed her lips as if she was going to say something important. Odette sighed and resigned herself to hearing it.

"It's not like I'm not going to miss you, Odette," Mieko began. "Summer is going to blow without you. And I can't believe you won't be there for seventh grade. But this is cool too, you know. You act like it's all so terrible, but you get to go on an adventure! And no more real school! That's pretty awesome, right?"

Odette either nodded or shrugged. She wasn't paying very close attention to what Mieko said, or to her own response. She'd been through it all, lots of times over the past three months—with Mieko, with her parents, with herself. They'd be getting the chance to have a good long visit with Grandma Sissy. They'd spend time together on the road. "*Real* time," Mom had said, as if all the time they'd spent in this house didn't count.

Opportunity, adventure, freedom. Blah, blah, blah.

Odette watched a lady and her teenage son load her family's television into the back of a minivan and wondered how much they'd paid for it. Then she saw her mom pocket three dollars in exchange for the blue vase. At least the high-ponytail lady wasn't buying it. It was Mrs. Murdoch, their neighbor two doors down.

But then that made Odette kind of mad, even though Mrs. Murdoch was a widow whose kids barely ever visited. "Don't you think that sucks?" she said to Mieko. "That our own neighbors are talking my parents down on stuff? I mean, they all know my dad lost his job and that we're selling our house. They've *seen* the Coach that we're moving into. And still Mrs. Murdoch wants to pay three dollars instead of five for a vase?"

"I guess." Mieko scratched a mosquito bite on her knee.

"But probably they're not thinking about you guys, you know? I mean, everyone wants a deal at a yard sale."

"Yeah," said Odette. She felt the sting of tears behind her eyes.

"Up, up, up, girls," said Dad. He was grinning and held a fold of bills in his hand. "Those chairs are now the property of this nice woman."

Odette groaned. High-ponytail lady stood just behind Odette's father, tapping her sneaker on the brick path. "Can you load them into the back of my car?"

"Will do," said Dad. "Come on, girls, give me a hand."

Really? It was too much to ask of her. But Odette stood and grabbed one side of the blue toile armchair. Mieko hefted the other, and together they crab-walked to the lady's car. It was one of those ridiculous, overpowered SUVs built for off-roading or safaris or something, but Odette would bet it had never left the wide highways of Orange County, California, except for the occasional weekend trip to Big Bear or Vegas.

When the chairs were loaded and the lady had driven away, Odette's dad said, "Hey, Mieko, stick around and help out for the afternoon, why don't you? I'll pay you twenty bucks."

Mieko grinned. "Sure, Simon!"

"*Et tu, Brute?*" mumbled Odette, too soft for Mieko to hear. They'd watched *Julius Caesar* in Language Arts just a few weeks ago, and that line had stuck with her. It was the last thing Caesar said as he was being assassinated —to his best friend, Brutus, who stuck a knife in him along with everyone else. It meant, "You too, Brutus?"

If Julius Caesar had come back as a zombie, like in a sequel or something, Odette wondered if he'd go after Brutus or if he'd just be too bummed to even try. If he'd just wander aimlessly, zombie leg dragging, away from everyone.

THE SALE WENT on until close to five p.m., when at last the traffic had dwindled to the occasional drive-by. All the furniture had sold; Rex had found a home for his whole box of Cubes for the tidy sum of thirty-five dollars (taking a ginormous loss, Odette figured, as there were a dozen Cubes, each costing $15.95 plus tax, but no one wanted to hear *that*); and then Mieko rode home, waving cheerily, a twenty-dollar bill tucked into her back pocket.

"I feel lighter and lighter," Odette heard Mom telling

Dad. He was reboxing loose plates and cups, getting ready to take a load to the thrift store.

"Me too," he said, and his smile looked genuine, even though his eyes were tired. "Lighter and lighter." He set down the box and then they kissed, and Odette watched, even though she wanted to look away. She couldn't remember ever seeing her parents like this—all kissy and huggy and touching nonstop. It was so *gross,* the way they were acting like all of this was a good thing. Like they weren't losing everything, like they weren't just throwing their lives away—and Odette's, too.

"Detters," said Mom when the kiss ended. "Want to go with your dad to drop off the leftovers at the thrift store?"

"No way," she answered, turning away before the tears spilled. The yard looked terrible—the grass was flattened where blankets full of clothes had been spread, and half-empty cardboard boxes littered the driveway.

Her parents felt lighter and lighter, thought Odette. But all she felt, watching her life disappear piece by piece into the arms of strangers—was emptier and emptier.

Consolation Prize

THE INSIDE OF the house looked a lot like the front lawn—decimated. That was a word Odette had learned recently too, in the same class that had introduced her to Julius Caesar. It meant "destroyed," but the old meaning was cooler—it was related to the root word *dec,* meaning "ten," and to decimate used to mean to randomly kill every tenth soldier. Or in this case, thought Odette as she scanned the bare walls, the empty outlets, the sad indented carpet squares where furniture had been, it was more like killing *nine* soldiers out of every ten. If she was lucky, maybe they'd leave this house with one-tenth of their possessions stashed in the Coach.

Odette went for a run around the block just to get away for a few minutes. She imagined her house behind her, the front lawn littered with dead soldiers and smashed cardboard boxes. She flat-out ran, not pacing herself or anything, but the problem with running around a block was that halfway around it she wasn't running *away* from her house anymore . . . she was running *toward* it. When she realized this, her arms dropped like weights to her sides and her run fizzled out into a reluctant trudge.

Mom got a pizza for dinner, which they ate on paper plates, since all the real plates were gone and the plastic camping dishes she'd ordered online for the Coach hadn't arrived yet. Dad was taking forever with the thrift store run, and Odette ate as much pizza as she could, trying to make sure that there wasn't enough left for him.

But after the third slice, her stomach started hurting. There was still plenty left for Dad, unfortunately. Still he wasn't home. Mom called him once and texted him a few times, but it was fully dark before Odette heard the rattle of his key unlocking the front door.

"Hello, hello," he called in the way he did, and Odette couldn't help but be relieved that he was there, even though she was angry at him for everything, even though she'd tried to eat all his pizza.

When Dad came into the kitchen, where Odette, Rex, and Mom were sitting at a folding card table (the kitchen table and benches had been among the first things to go),

Odette was surprised to see that he held a box. A cardboard box, just like the ones Odette had grown so tired of seeing in the hallways of the house, on their front porch. But the look on Dad's face . . . *that* was different.

"What've you got there, Simon?" asked Mom.

Dad smiled, but he looked guilty, the way his forehead wrinkled up. "Don't be mad," he said. "It's something for Odette."

And before Dad said another word, before her mom even answered, Odette knew with one hundred percent certainty what was in that box.

It was her puppy. Her dream puppy. The dog she'd wanted for as long as she had known about puppies. A sleek black seal of a dog, with floppy ears and a long pink tongue and a tail that wagged its whole butt. A Labrador retriever that she could train to run by her side even off-leash, who'd learn to sit and stay and would sleep heavy by her feet, a strong protector and warrior.

And then the box whined and moved—not the box, but what was inside—and Odette's one hundred percent certainty doubled, and maybe this was all worth it, losing their house and leaving school and having to live in a dumb ugly Coach with no privacy and a bathroom smaller than a closet, if she would be doing it with a Labrador puppy named Francis.

"Simon," said Mom, and her voice sounded surprised more than angry. Then Dad put the box on the table and motioned for Odette to open it. Rex, of course, lunged across the table to be the first to see inside the box, but Dad stopped him.

"This is for Odette," he said. And then, "Go ahead, honey. Open the box."

Her hands trembled. Her *lips* trembled. The box trembled. Odette pulled back on the cardboard flap. But before she got it all the way open, a wet black nose nudged against her hand, insisting on freedom, pushing the box open from the inside. And then—

Out poured the ugliest little runt of a dog Odette had ever seen.

It was an abomination. Black, yes, as she'd imagined, but not shiny. Dull wiry hair stuck out at every angle from its skinny little body—it couldn't have weighed more than three or four pounds. Its snout pointed sharp and eager. It made a sound like *Yap!*—high and shrill.

"What *is* it?" asked Rex, amazed.

"It's a dog, of course," said Dad. "Odette's dog."

Burning tears blurred her vision. "I don't want it," she said, and shoved the box away. But the dog yapped again, closely followed by a string of *yips*, and it jumped out of the box and onto her lap. Its tiny paws were poky and terrible. Its foxlike face stared up at her. And then Odette's lap began to feel moist and warm.

"It *peed* on me," she screeched, and thrust the creature in her mom's direction. And as she ran to her room—or what was left of it, after the morning's yard sale decimation—Odette heard the cacophony of her family behind her, and yip upon yip from that terrible little dog.

Good Home Needed

I'M SURE SHE didn't *mean* to pee on you."

Odette ignored her mother. They were her favorite jeans, one of just three pairs she planned to take with her on the road. And now they smelled like musty dog pee.

"I can't believe Dad brought that *thing* home," she muttered, more to herself than to her mother, as she held her jeans under the faucet in the bathroom.

"Try not to be so hard on him," Mom said. "He was trying to give you a gift—you've been harping on us to get you a dog for years."

Harping on them. Great. "When Rex wanted a ferret, you didn't even wait a week to get him one," Odette said. Her throat felt tight with tears, and her voice came out kind of soft. "Even though ferrets are illegal in California."

"*Technically* illegal," said Mom. "You can buy everything but the ferret at the pet store—food, bedding, toys.

And it's not the same thing, Detters. Rex's ferret sleeps in a cage. He's contained. A dog . . . that's a whole other thing. A big responsibility."

"Exactly," said Odette. She turned off the faucet and squeezed the water out of her jeans, then sat on the edge of the bathtub. "A dog *is* a big deal. So why would Dad go through all the trouble just to get me the wrong kind? You guys know I wanted a Lab."

Mom looked annoyed. Her hair frizzed out more than normal, as if she were generating electricity, and she had her arms folded across her chest. "A dog is a dog, Detters," she said. "Try to be more grateful. Besides," she added, turning to leave the bathroom, "there's no room for a great big Labrador in the Coach. The dog Dad brought home is travel-size."

At last she closed the door behind her, leaving Odette alone with her peed-on jeans and her tears and the hard, ungrateful feeling in her chest. As if that made it any better—that this dog was the perfect size for traveling cross-country in that ridiculous contraption.

Odette still hadn't even been inside the Coach. Rex had been popping in and out ever since their parents had driven it home two weeks ago, begging to sleep in it. Planning out how best to make use of the one cabinet that would be his storage space. Packing and repacking the plastic stackable boxes that would go in the side compartments. Telling his ferret, Paul, all about the trip they would be taking—how they were heading first to visit Grandma Sissy on a real-life island, how they'd get to watch movies while they drove, that there was a mini-refrigerator and a mini-stove in the Coach, for making real-live food.

But Odette refused to go inside. Not that it mattered. She knew there was no way out of this whole mess.

She cried for a while, but it didn't make her feel any better. Then she splashed cold water on her face, pulled on her robe, and opened the bathroom door to take her jeans to the washing machine.

Dad was standing in the hallway, one hand raised, poised to knock, with that dog tucked under his other arm. "There you are," he said, as if he didn't know she'd been in the bathroom the whole time. "Here," he said, holding the dog out to Odette. "Sorry she peed on you. The guy at the thrift store said she was house trained, so maybe she just got excited."

Odette stared at the dog. Its tail wagged for a second,

then went limp between its legs. "You got a dog at a thrift store?"

"Outside the thrift store," Dad said. "There was a guy there with a sign that said 'Good Home Needed.'"

"Then why did *you* take it?" Odette said, knowing how mean she sounded. "We don't even have a home." She pushed past her dad, ignoring the dog. "I've got to wash my jeans and see if I can get the pee out."

But Dad followed her to the laundry room. He watched her start the washing machine, pour in the detergent, and throw in her jeans. She added a bunch of other darks from the laundry basket so she wouldn't be wasting water, washing just one pair of jeans. He didn't say anything. It was like he was waiting for her to finish.

Which it turned out he was, because as soon as Odette loaded the washing machine, as soon as her hands were empty, Dad thrust the dog out in her direction. "She needs some dinner," Dad said. "And a name."

This time Odette took the dog, because Dad was blocking the doorway. The dog wriggled in her hands and licked the air in front of its face, like it was trying to kiss her but couldn't reach. "What kind of a dog is it, anyway?"

"It's a girl, not an it," Dad said. "Probably some kind of

a terrier. Look, honey, I know this wasn't the dog you had pictured. I know none of this is your vision. But think of it this way—you might not want this dog, but this dog needs you."

Odette sighed. She held the dog closer. Warm doggy breath panted into her face. She felt the dog's fast little heart thump against her own chest. It was still the ugliest dog she had ever seen. A scrap of a dog. Barely a dog at all.

"Okay," she said. "I'll feed the dog."

"And give her a name," Dad called after her as Odette headed to the kitchen.

She pretended not to hear him.

Barely a Dog

THE DOG DIDN'T want to sleep at the foot of Odette's bed—actually, Odette's mattress. The bed frame had been sold that morning. As soon as she set the dog there, it bounded up to the pillow and burrowed under her sheet and blankets, snuffing around along her legs and then settling in against her side.

When her parents came in to say good night, they looked around and then said, "Where's the dog?"

Odette pointed to her side, and her parents smiled all knowingly like, *We knew you'd love her once you gave her a chance,* but Odette didn't feel like she loved the dog. Tolerated, maybe, at best.

It was weird that her parents had come in together to kiss her good night. It used to be just Mom, since Dad worked late so often. Even on the weekends, when he wasn't working, it had always been one or the other of them tucking her in. Things were different lately. And different, to Odette, was not comfortable.

"Did you name her yet?" asked Mom.

"Nope."

"She looks like a Rosie," said Dad. "Or maybe Daisy?"

"She might barely be a dog, Dad, but she's not a flower." Odette heard the mean edge in her voice. It was there almost all the time these days, and she didn't like it, but she couldn't seem to cut it out. Besides, she wanted her parents to know that she was mad at them—that she didn't forgive them.

"I'm sure you'll think of something," Mom said, and she bent down to kiss Odette. Odette tolerated the kiss (the way she was tolerating the dog) but didn't return it. Her dad kissed her too, and stroked her hair back from her forehead. It felt nice, that touch, even though she didn't want it to. At her side, the dog sighed and stretched, as if she was experiencing some kind of blissful peace.

Mom turned the lights out as they left, and shut the door halfway. Odette lay awake in the darkness, her eyes open. One of her hands curled around the dog's little body. She could feel every tiny rib. The dog had gobbled down the lunch meat Odette had put in a bowl for her, as if she hadn't eaten in days. They'd have to go to the pet store tomorrow to get her some real dog food.

And a leash and a collar, thought Odette.

All she had was two more nights. Two more nights in this room, the room where she'd slept her whole life. And then they would be gone.

Ready to Roll

ON JUNE FIFTH, at six o'clock in the evening, Mom revved the engine of the Coach. Rex was already inside, and Paul the ferret was nested into his hammock. Dad circled the Coach, doing a final inspection, making sure their bikes were secure on the rack, double-checking the locks on all the side compartments.

They had planned to head out by noon, and it seemed a bad omen to Odette that even before the trip was under way they were already behind schedule. Someone had left the lights in the Coach on all night, probably Rex, though he swore he'd switched everything off, and the battery was drained dead. Dad decided that it was kind of an old battery anyway, so they might as well replace it, but then he'd had to go to three places to find the right one for an RV.

Friends and gawkers from the neighborhood dotted

the sidewalk. The nine-year-old twins from across the street had made a WE'LL MISS YOU, ZYSKOWSKI FAMILY sign, and they'd even spelled it right, but it was taking so long for the Coach to pull away that they'd dropped the sign to the grass and were climbing the willow tree.

Odette stood with Mieko just at the edge of the brick path that led to their house. No—it truly wasn't their house anymore. At eight o'clock that morning, the Waldmans had become proud homeowners. The contract stipulated that the Zyskowski family now had three days to vacate the property, but at this point even Odette didn't want to draw it out any further. It was like peeling off the slowest, stickiest Band-Aid in the world.

"I can't believe you're really leaving," Mieko said. "I mean, of course you're leaving, but, like, I can't believe you're not coming back."

"We might come back," Odette said. "My parents never said we weren't coming back for sure." Technically, this was true, but with all the layers of problems, with no home to come back to and Grandma Sissy being sick and the trouble between her parents . . . a return did not seem likely.

Mieko nodded. "It sucks that you don't even have your own cell phone anymore."

This was almost too painful to discuss. Her parents had warned her a while ago that they'd be canceling her cell phone plan and Dad's before they headed out on the road. "Why do four people living in one recreational vehicle need three separate phones?" Odette's mother had said. "We'll be together all the time. We can share one phone. One family phone."

Rex had been stoked by this news—he'd had no phone before, and now he technically owned one-quarter of their single family cell phone. But Odette was infuriated.

"I can't believe you're doing this to me!" she'd said—actually, she'd yelled—when, that morning, she found that her phone didn't work anymore. The little black mutt, who followed Odette everywhere, tangling up between her feet and tripping her up, had cowered at the sound of Odette's anger, tucking her tail under her rump and whining.

"You're going to be a lot happier, honey, when you understand that not everything is about you," Dad had said, but that certainly didn't help *at all*.

"I know they're not *trying* to ruin my life," Odette said to Mieko.

"But if they *were*," Mieko answered, her eyes darting all over the Jamboree, "they'd be off to a pretty good start."

It was okay that Mieko said that kind of stuff out loud. It was good, actually. Like having a second mouth when hers felt too overwhelmed to speak, a second brain to take over when her own felt like it had dealt with all it could handle.

"You have the new number programmed into your phone?"

Mieko nodded. Odette knew she would—it was just something to say—and suddenly she was ready to climb into the Coach. Even driving away seemed easier than this, easier than saying goodbye.

So when Dad finished circling the Jamboree and put his hand on her shoulder, saying, "Ready to roll, hon?" Odette didn't argue. She just hugged Mieko.

"Call every day," she said, and Mieko answered, "You too."

Odette followed Dad up the two metal stairs and pulled the door shut behind her, a tinny slam of finality. She slid into the bench seat across from Rex and fastened her seat belt. The scrawny runt dog had been waiting for her, and it jumped up and licked her face, scratching her arms with its sharp black claws. Odette didn't care that it hurt.

Then the Coach was rolling down the street, her mom honking, Rex waving like a king, all the neighbors cheering, and there, through the window, was Mieko on her bike, pedaling alongside them, right on the other side of the glass. She pedaled hard and stood up, the way she did, and smiled big.

And it was nice, in that moment, with the neighbors and Mieko, and Mom honking and Rex all excited across from her. But then they turned the corner at the end of the street, toward the highway, and of course Mieko couldn't follow, and the neighbors' cheers faded away, and even Rex and the rat dog settled down, and then it was quiet except for the engine, and there was nothing but the impossibly long road still to come.

All Downhill

THE MILES SPILLED out behind them like an unrolling spool of thread. Traffic through Los Angeles was terrible, stop and go for a good two hours, and then came the Grapevine, the long, windy road that stretched over the San Gabriel Mountains. Mom kept the Coach in the slow lane along with the big trucks. Smaller, sleeker vehicles swooshed by in the left lane.

"We'll find a place to stop when we get to the other side of the Grapevine," Dad said. He sat shotgun next to Mom, whose shoulders had that tense look, raised up a little, her elbows tucked against her sides as she drove.

"I'm bored," said Rex, casting aside his Game-X, and though it was the first time he'd said these words, Odette felt certain that it wouldn't be the last.

"Congratulations," she said to him. "You made it a

whole three hours before getting bored. That's three hours longer than I made it."

"You're always bored," answered Rex, which wasn't true at all, and was totally unfair.

"I'm only bored when I'm stuck with you," said Odette.

Rex made an obscene hand gesture, but he flashed it so quickly that Odette couldn't be sure it was what she thought it was. Then he laughed in quick, short barks, in a way that he knew made Odette angry. Next to her, half asleep, the little black dog growled softly. Apparently she didn't like Rex's laugh either.

"It'll be your responsibility to feed her and walk her," Mom had said the morning after Dad gave Odette the wrong dog. "And of course to clean up after her."

At first Odette had been surprised that the dog already seemed to know that the right place to poop and pee was outside, but then Dad told her, "She's not a puppy, after all."

"She's not? You mean, she's not going to get *any* bigger?"

"I don't think so."

Dogs were supposed to be big. Like big, strong, cuddly bears.

Across from her, Rex was doing that thing again where he picked at the skin around his fingernails. It drove Odette so crazy, she could hardly stand it. It made her want to scream, or pull out her hair, or slap Rex's hands away from each other.

In her head, Odette started a list.

Things That Aren't Fair:
1. Living in the Coach.
2. Getting the Wrong Dog.
3. Having Rex for a brother.
4. Sharing one stupid cell phone.

The Coach chugged along.

"This is the summit!" Mom sounded happy. Relieved, maybe, that the Coach had made it to the top of the Grapevine.

"It's all downhill from here," Dad said.

Quietly, to herself, Odette whispered, "That's what I'm afraid of."

The Red One

I T WAS NEARLY eleven p.m. by the time Mom pulled the Coach into a small campsite just past Bakersfield, in a town called Buttonwillow. First, of course, Odette had to take the dog out to pee, and as she waited in the cool, breezy night, she wondered sleepily if that might make a decent name for a dog—Buttonwillow. Or maybe just Button, or Willow.

It didn't really matter. She could name the dog nothing, or anything at all. It wouldn't change a thing.

Back in the Coach, Odette found her parents tucking Rex into his bed, which was where they'd been sitting —the bench seats and table collapsed together and folded into a bed. With the table converted into a bed, there was even less space for maneuvering around.

At the back of the Coach was her parents' bed. It was

a queen, the same size they'd had at home, so they'd kept their old bedding. It looked strange here, on this lower mattress, in this smaller space, the quilt reaching all the way to the floor, pooling on the brownish carpet. On either side of the bed, a little lamp jutted out from the back wall, just at the right height for reading. Under the mattress, Odette knew, were some pull-out plastic boxes filled with books and a second set of sheets.

There was a curtain—a privacy screen, Mom had called it—that separated the big bed from the rest of the Coach. Then there was the door to the tiny bathroom, and a little closet across from it. After that was the kitchen, with a miniature fridge, a metal sink, a stove with two burners, and an oven that looked big enough to cook a frozen dinner but not much else.

The table/bed where Rex was falling asleep was just across from the door. At the very front were the "captain's chair," as Mom called the driver's seat, and the "navigator's nook," as she called the spot where Dad had sat.

Mom loved to name things.

And up above the front two seats was Odette's "room." While Odette was outside with the dog, her parents had pulled out the ladder from the closet and leaned it so she could get up to her bed, and Odette saw that one of them—probably Mom—had turned on the light up there and folded back the blanket in an attempt to make it look homier.

Odette had already used the bathroom, and she figured it would be easier to sleep in her T-shirt and jeans than to bother changing, so she dumped the dog on Rex's feet and climbed the ladder. She switched off the light and turned her back on her parents, closing her eyes against tears.

A minute later she felt Mom's cool touch on her forehead, followed by a kiss. "We love you, Detters," Mom said.

Then she felt Dad pat her leg through the blankets. "You forgot someone," he said, and deposited the dog by the crook of her knee. "Sweet dreams."

The dog circled and snuffed around, and finally flopped down. Her little body felt warm to Odette, even through the blanket.

She lay there and listened to her parents open a bottle of wine, listened to them whisper as they took it outside. She listened to the deep, nasally breathing of her little brother, and the softer, more shallow breaths of the dog behind her knees. She listened to the hum of the highway not far away, and she listened to her own pitiful sobs against her pillow—the one throw pillow she had chosen. The red one.

Number five, she added to her list, wiping her eyes against the pillow. *The throw pillows I had to leave behind.*

Donut Holes

WHEN ODETTE WOKE, the dog was right up by her face, asleep with her doggy head on Odette's pillow, her little body tucked under the covers, breathing into Odette's nose soft, warm puffs of air. The dog's wiry black hair stuck out at every angle, and Odette smoothed it back away from her closed eyes. The dog yawned. Her pink tongue stretched out, her tiny white teeth shined. Then she slowly opened her eyes—deep black pearls.

Down below, Dad was pulling out the coffee pot. He filled it with water from a refillable canister beneath the sink and spooned ground coffee into the top part. Then he plugged the whole thing in and turned it on. It was a full-size coffeemaker, even in their pint-size kitchen, because Odette's parents "believed" in coffee. It looked ridiculous and oversize on the narrow countertop, leaving barely any room for anything else. Also, totally unfair—her parents got a full-size coffeemaker and Odette had to get rid of almost all her pillows. Even though Odette "believed" in throw pillows.

Odette could see a lump in the big bed at the back of the Coach. Mom was still sleeping, and Rex must have crawled in with their parents in the middle of the night, as he often did, because his table bed was empty.

The dog got up and stretched, circling on the bed and snuffling around.

"Good morning, honey," Dad whispered. "How'd you sleep?"

"So-so," said Odette, though she'd slept as deeply and well as she could ever remember.

"Looks like your dog needs to go out," Dad said. "Do you want me to take her for you? You could sleep a little longer."

But Odette was wide awake. "No, that's all right," she said. "I'll take her." She sat up and hit her head on the top of the Coach.

"Ooh," said Dad.

Odette rubbed her head and climbed down the ladder.

Then she reached up and grabbed the dog, who wagged her tail fiercely.

"Put on her harness," Dad said, which Odette was planning to do anyway. She'd hung it on a hook by the door the night before. The dog struggled like a piglet as Odette fit her into the harness, shoving her head through the big loop and pushing her pointy little front legs through their spaces. Then she clipped the whole thing together and attached the leash.

"Don't forget a bag," Dad whisper-called after Odette as she pushed open the door. She hadn't; one of the green biodegradable poop bags Mom had bought at the pet store along with the harness and the dog food was already tucked into Odette's pocket from last night.

The dog leaped down the two pop-out stairs, landing squarely and romping off, stretching the leash tight. Odette followed after, surprised by the warmth of the morning air that greeted her. They'd only traveled a few hours from home, but already the weather had changed.

It was an ugly campground. The night before, it had been too dark to see clearly, but this morning Odette took in all the ugly around her—the few squat tents set up on patches of dirt-bare earth, the bathroom building down the way with its peeling paint and wooden block letters announcing WOMEN and MEN.

Trees lined the perimeter, separating the campground from the road just beyond. They looked thirsty, those trees, underwatered and sad.

The dog squatted and peed in the dirt, but the ground was so dry that the pee couldn't even soak in. It pooled in the dust, running downhill toward Odette's foot.

"Is that your dog?"

Odette turned around. There behind her, poking her head out from the biggest of the tents, was a girl. "I guess," Odette answered.

"She's so cute!"

She was one of those girls who gushed. Odette watched as she unzipped the tent the rest of the way and crawled out, and then Odette tried not to stare, because it was rude to stare, but it was hard not to. The girl's hair was wild, too wild to have gotten that way just from sleeping on the ground a couple of nights.

It was a giant cloud of light brown fluff. It was an aura of hair.

"What's her name?"

"Um," said Odette. She didn't want to tell this girl that she still hadn't come up with a name. "Georgette," she blurted out, the first name that popped into her head.

"Cute," the girl said again. "What's *your* name?"

"Odette," Odette said.

"Odette and Georgette. Adorable."

"But I call her Georgie," Odette amended. "No one calls her Georgette." This last part, at least, was true.

"Well, I'm Katie," said the girl. She squatted down to pet the dog now named Georgie. Katie's legs were long and skinny, with dry white scratches up and down them. She wasn't wearing any shoes. "Good girl," she crooned. She reached out and the dog waggled her butt and scooted, low to the ground, toward Katie's hand.

"This is, like, the smallest dog I've ever seen," said Katie. "What kind is she?"

"I don't know," said Odette. "Some mutt." Her attention was divided between Katie, who was now scratching Georgie's belly, the dog having rolled onto her back in the dirt, and Katie's tent, from which someone else was emerging. It was a woman, with hair just like Katie's, but bigger.

"Is that your mom?" Odette asked.

"Uh-huh," said Katie, not bothering to look back. "I wish I had a dog."

For a second, Odette considered offering the runt to her.

Then Katie's mom called, "Hey, girls! Do you want some donuts?"

Katie gave Georgie one final scratch and then stood. "Sure," she answered. Then, to Odette, "You want some?"

Odette shrugged. She wasn't supposed to take food from strangers, but this seemed like a safe exception.

Katie's mom pulled a blue and white box from the trunk of their car, a beat-up old hatchback parked just beyond their tent.

"Thanks," Odette said. She looked into the box. Actually, there weren't any donuts. The box was filled with little round powdered balls—donut holes, not donuts. But, Odette figured, it was close enough.

They sat on a couple of big logs that had been upended to make stools and ate the donut holes. The sun shone hot on the back of Odette's neck. Georgie tucked into the patch of shade behind Odette's knees and flopped down, panting.

"So where are you from?" Katie broke her donut

holes into little pieces before eating them. It was a good technique; no powdered sugar dusted her chin.

"Not that far from here," Odette said. "Just Southern California."

"That's where we're headed," Katie said. "We live near Sacramento. We're going to Disneyland."

Odette nodded. Aside from the beaches, Disneyland was the biggest attraction near her house. "We used to have yearly passes," she said.

"No way!" Katie seemed impressed. "You mean, you could just go whenever you wanted to?"

"There were a bunch of blackout dates, like around holidays. And Saturdays, too. But we could go on Sundays. Sometimes we'd go just for a couple of hours after school."

"That's so awesome!" said Katie. "How come you don't have passes anymore?"

Odette cleared her throat. She'd inhaled some powdered sugar from her last bite. "We don't really live there anymore," she said.

"Oh," said Katie. "Where *do* you live?"

Suddenly Odette was embarrassed. She kind of shrugged, and then pointed at the Coach. "There, for now," she said.

"Really?"

"Yeah, for now. We're kind of . . . I don't know, traveling around, I guess."

"Cool," said Katie. "Where are you going?"

"Well, we're going to go see my Grandma Sissy first," Odette said. "Because she's sick." Odette felt a funny discomfort in her belly, thinking of Grandma Sissy being sick. She'd been sick before, and she'd gotten better then. So there was no reason to think that she wouldn't get better this time too.

"And then what?"

Odette shrugged. "Mom says the world is our oyster."

"Huh," Katie said. Then, "What about school?"

"Mom says we're roadschooling."

"What?"

"You know. Like homeschooling, but on the road. She says we're going to 'live our education.'"

"Huh," said Katie again. "That's pretty crazy."

"Yeah."

"What about, like, work? And money and stuff?"

The more she got into it, the less Odette felt like sharing, but Katie's face didn't look judgmental or anything, just curious. "My dad got laid off from his job," she said.

"Is that, like, fired?"

Odette shook her head. "No. Fired means you did something wrong. Laid off just means . . . I don't know, that they don't need you anymore."

"Oh," Katie said, and she nodded, but her expression looked like she felt sorry for Odette or something, for having a dad whose job didn't need him.

"It was kind of heroic, actually," Odette blurted. "See, Dad used to make kind of a lot of money. We had a big house and everything. But his work was going to lay off a bunch of guys who made less than he did. So my dad, what he did was, he offered to leave instead. So that three other guys could keep their jobs." She left out the other part, the part that she still hadn't told her parents she'd overheard. About "the trouble we've been having with us" and how Dad figured it couldn't make things any worse.

"Huh," said Katie. "So, your dad saved their jobs . . . but now you guys don't have a house?"

Odette stood up. She forgot she was holding Georgie's leash and she sort of yanked it. The dog yipped a little. "I've got to go," said Odette. "Thanks for the donut holes."

No Privacy

"D ID YOU MAKE a friend?" Mom asked.

Inside the Coach, everyone was awake and eating breakfast, Rex's bed converted back into a table.

"I don't have any friends," Odette answered. She looked around, for somewhere—anywhere—to be alone. The only door in the whole stupid Coach was to the bathroom, so she headed there, depositing Georgie on Dad's lap.

Odette shut the flimsy door and locked it behind her, closed the toilet lid, and sat down. The walls were getting closer and tighter. They must be. Was the bathroom *always* this small? As she sat on the toilet, her knees reached halfway across the bathroom. She didn't even want to *think* about what it must be like for her dad, with his long, skinny legs—bird legs, Mom called them—when he had to use the toilet.

Odette closed her eyes to make the bathroom go

away. She tried to take deep breaths and count to ten, but she only made it to six before she heard a scratching sound from inside the little shower cube just across from the toilet.

It could be a zombie. Maybe that's why the Coach was for sale in the first place. Maybe it was zombie-infested.

Odette opened her eyes. She stood up and squared her shoulders. She pulled back the shower curtain.

It wasn't a zombie. It was Rex's ferret, a long white tube of a creature, snuffling around by the shower drain. Above him hung his green and white striped hammock, attached to the shower walls by suction cups.

Odette had forgotten that Dad set the ferret up in here. "This way," he'd said, "when we make a sharp turn or hit a bump, the ferret won't slip and slide. He'll just rock in the hammock like a baby."

Even in the bathroom of the Coach, Odette wasn't entirely alone.

She pushed open the little door. In the kitchenette, Mom flipped pancakes on the stovetop.

Rex, beside her, supervised. "It's bubbling. Flip it, flip it, flip it."

"Relax, buddy." Mom slid the spatula beneath the

pancake and turned it over. It sizzled when it hit the pan. "Detters," Mom said. "Get the syrup out of the fridge, will you, and heat some up in the microwave."

"Why can't Rex do it?"

"It's sticky," Rex said, rolling up on the balls of his feet.

"I don't even *want* pancakes."

"Just get the syrup out, okay?"

Odette wanted to say no, it was not okay. No, she would not get the syrup. No, no, no.

But instead, she got the syrup. Even though it was completely unfair.

What Friends Are

THEY WERE ON the road again an hour later. Dad drove this time, and Mom set out the magnetic chess set. She and Rex played tournament-style, with a little timer monitoring how long they took for each turn. Odette sat next to Rex, attempting to read.

She tried to fold her legs up on the bench seat, but the table was too close. Though she managed to wiggle one knee up, it got stuck, and when she stretched her leg back down, her knee banged against the bottom of the table, rattling the chessboard.

"Good thing Odette's not stronger than the magnets," Rex said, his eyes like magnets themselves, transfixed on the little plastic chess pieces that wobbled but did not tip.

Mom laughed. Odette held back the impulse to shove him. It was *so annoying* how he always had a comment for everything, often mean-sounding, and how Mom always laughed. If Odette ever said anything like the things Rex said, Mom would protest, "Oh, Odette. Be nice."

Odette knew it was because Rex hadn't started talking until he was almost three. She remembered how worried her parents had been about that. And when he finally *did* begin to speak, in grammatically perfect sentences full of fancy words, Mom and Dad had been so grateful that *what* he said hardly seemed to matter.

It was Rex's turn. Odette could see from the board that he was closing in on Mom's queen. It was just a matter of time. Mom probably knew it too, but losing never seemed to bother her the way it bothered Odette.

She looked up at Odette and gave her a *sympathetic look*. "Want to talk about it?"

"No," said Odette. She flipped the page of her book even though she'd only read half of it.

"You know," said Mom, talking anyway, "there are lots of kinds of friendships. Some last forever, some are situational. And that's okay. Not all friendships have to look the same."

"Uh-huh." Now Odette couldn't even make out the

words of the page she was pretending to read; tears blurred her vision.

"Like, you might have one set of friends for surviving high school, and another set entirely for going skiing with."

"They're not friends if you're just using them to get through things or just to hang out with," said Odette without looking up. "That's not what friends are."

"Ah," said Mom. She moved her rook in a noble attempt to protect her queen. The chess pieces, Odette thought, moved an awful lot like zombies. Slowly and deliberately, rarely in more than one direction at a time.

"Sometimes a friend can be someone you don't know for very long, but someone you connect with anyway. Someone who comes into your life and then leaves it," Mom said.

"Check," said Rex. He hadn't looked up from the board the whole time.

"You little rascal," said Mom, but she sounded proud. Not mad.

"I don't want any friends that I can't keep around," said Odette.

"You might need to expand your definition." Mom made a last-ditch effort to save her king, moving her queen to block a castle that threatened it. But it was too little too late.

Rex didn't even hesitate to knock the queen out of the way. Two moves later it was all over. "Checkmate," he said.

Fun and Games

ODETTE WATCHED THE long, flat, boring landscape speed by. It actually didn't matter if they were going sixty miles an hour or if they weren't moving at all. The view didn't change, for hours, in any discernible way. Dry, dead hills. Green-gray scrub bushes here and there. Car after car speeding by in the other direction, toward somewhere better. Flat asphalt highway, shimmering like a mirage in the heat of midafternoon.

"It's a hundred and two out there," Dad told them from the captain's chair, and then, a second later, out of nowhere a loud sound burst—*POW!*—like a shotgun. Rex screamed and Georgie fell off Odette's lap as the Coach swerved hard to the right, and then, as Dad called, "Hang on!" and cranked the steering wheel to the left, Odette felt the rear of the Coach fishtailing in response.

THUNK THUNK THUNK came a rhythmic beat from

underneath the front of the Coach, and Mom yelled, "Easy on the brakes, Simon, just keep her straight," and Dad yelled, "I'm trying, Liz," and there it was—that tone Odette hadn't heard from either of her parents lately, that tone they used to use with each other all the time, sharp and hard and not very nice—and Rex had his hands over his ears and kept screaming. Georgie scrambled around in the kitchenette, her little claws unable to grab hold because of the smooth fake wood flooring, and Odette gripped the edge of the table with both hands.

"Keep the wheel straight, Simon, or you'll tip us over," Mom barked out, and Odette found herself wishing that Mom were in the captain's chair instead of Dad. She was bossy sometimes, but she didn't mess around.

Dad's hands on the wheel were white-knuckled, but he managed to hold the Coach steady. His foot pumped hard on the brake, and gradually they slowed. He pulled over to the emergency lane and they finally stopped. With a shaking hand, Dad turned the key in the ignition.

The *THUNK THUNK THUNK* sound had been so loud that now the silence in the Coach felt eerie.

"What happened?" asked Odette. Her whole body felt shaky and weak.

"Tire blowout," Dad said. His hands still gripped the steering wheel, but he turned his head to smile at them at the table. "It's okay," he said. "We're okay."

But the Coach tilted to the right, and without the air conditioning running, the day's heat was quickly invading, and they were in the middle of nowhere and the whole place stank of cow poop.

Definitely not okay.

"We have a spare tire," Dad said.

"And a jack," Mom said. "In the side compartment."

They all clambered out. Rex shoved sleepy Paul into his pouch—a purse thing made out of mesh that Rex wore around his neck—and the ferret wound into a ball and immediately fell back to sleep. Odette clipped the leash to Georgie's harness. It was too hot to leave the animals inside.

The Coach cast a long rectangular shadow onto the hard-packed dirt at the side of the road. Mom told Odette, "Keep your brother right here."

A big rig hauling two open white bins overfilled with tomatoes sped by, sending up a rush of hot air in its wake.

Odette thought about setting Georgie down, but the

ground felt hot even through her shoes, so she kept the dog in her arms. She put one hand on Rex's shoulder.

"Don't," he said, but she didn't move her hand. He tried to shrug it off for a minute but then got distracted when Mom opened the Coach's side compartment and started digging through all the stuff, searching for the jack.

"I don't know why you packed it so far in the back, Simon," Mom said. There it was again—her old irritated tone. She yanked out a bin full of sports equipment—balls and mitts and wetsuits—and it spilled open when it toppled on its side.

Odette let go of Rex's shoulder so she could help Mom put the stuff back in the bin, but Mom barked at her, "Stay with your brother!"

Fine. If that was how she wanted it.

At last Mom found the jack, shoved way into the deepest corner of the compartment. Dad managed to wrangle the spare tire out from underneath the back of the RV, and he rolled it toward them.

"Watch and learn," he said with a smile, but it looked forced.

If it hadn't been so hot and miserable, the whole thing might have been funny—Dad wrestling with the heavy tire, Mom straining to loosen the lug nuts, the two of them shoving the jack under the axle and trying to figure out how to make it work. It took forever.

"Why do you think the tire blew?" Mom asked Dad as they struggled to pull off the old tire. It was shredded, the long rubber length of it loose and floppy.

"Maybe we hit something," Dad said. "Those big trucks throw all kinds of stuff onto the road."

Finally they managed to take off the old tire, fit the new tire onto the axle, and crank tight all the lug nuts that would hold it in place.

"There we go," Dad said, sounding pleased. "We did it." And he decompressed the hydraulic jack to lower the Coach back to the ground.

They all watched together as the Coach's weight descended onto the new tire. For one moment it looked perfect . . . but then the tire began to deflate. The Coach listed again to the right, a sad, tippy mess.

"You've got to be kidding," Mom muttered. Her eyes were red-rimmed and her hair was a mess. "A flat spare? Really?"

They had to call a tow truck. It was too hot to wait outside, so they climbed back into the Coach and ran the engine so they could use the air conditioning. Rex held Paul in front of the vent and blasted the cold air right in his face. The ferret sniffed the air like it was the best thing he had ever smelled.

More than an hour passed before help arrived.

The tow truck guy's name was Louis. It said so right on his grease-stained blue shirt. "Didja remember to check the tire pressure every time you filled up?" he asked, first thing.

"Um," said Dad.

"You've gotta keep an eye on tire pressure, in this heat," Louis said. "If the pressure's low, the sidewalls can overheat and the tread just comes right off."

"Or we could have run over something," Dad said. He seemed irritated.

"Could be," Louis said. "No way to know."

He had an air compressor in his truck, so after he jacked the Coach back up, he pumped the spare tire full. Everyone clambered back outside to watch him work. "There you go," he said. Everything he did looked easy—the way he placed the jack, the smooth crank of his wrist as he twisted off the cap to insert the air compressor's hose.

Professional, Odette thought. This was a guy who knew what he was doing. Not like her dad.

"You folks be careful out here." Louis handed a clipboard to Mom with an invoice for her to sign. "Folks think it's all fun and games to drive one of these babies, but lots of things can go wrong."

"We appreciate your concern," Dad said drily. Mom handed back the clipboard with a tight smile.

After Louis drove away, honking cheerily, Mom took the keys from Dad's hand. "Let me drive for a while," she said.

Rolling Boil

"DO YOU THINK this is hot enough?" Dad asked, lifting the pot's lid and peering inside.

"Is it boiling?"

Steam fogged Dad's glasses. "I don't know," he said. "Sort of."

"Is it a rolling boil?"

"That sounds like an infection," Odette said from her nook. "A really gross infection. A case of the rolling boils."

No one heard her.

"If it's not a rolling boil, the pasta won't cook well." Mom's voice sounded like at least a simmer.

"I don't know, Liz, it looks good enough to me."

"Good enough to you isn't necessarily good enough," Mom said.

Odette looked across the Coach to the big bed in the back, where Rex sat cross-legged, ears covered by the massive headphones he insisted on wearing instead of earbuds, his thumbs twitching across the keys of his Game-X. He looked totally oblivious to the thunderstorm of energy in the kitchenette.

But you never could tell, with Rex. It could seem like he was off and away, spiraled up tight like a roly-poly bug, but that didn't mean he didn't know what was going on.

Dad thrust the spaghetti sticks into the water, apparently tired of waiting for a rolling boil. Mom's shoulders clenched up tight, something Odette knew she herself had inherited.

The whole inside of the Coach felt like that pot, and they were the spaghetti sticks. Pushed together, too tight, too hot.

Suddenly the water boiled and foamed up, spilling over the sides of the pot, hissing and splashing as it met the electric coils.

"Careful, Simon!" The irritation in Mom's voice made the whole Coach feel even smaller, even tighter.

Odette hopped down from her nook and headed outside. Georgie yipped and tried to follow, but Odette shoved her back inside and closed the door.

LATER, THEY ATE overcooked spaghetti and sauce from a jar. They sat jammed tight in the little booth because outside a swarm of wasps circled hungrily.

"It'd make a great name for a band," Rex said suddenly, twirling his fork in his bowl.

"What would, buddy?" Mom asked.

"Rolling Boil," Rex answered. Both Mom and Dad laughed, too loud, Odette thought. Her joke had been way better, and no one had said a thing.

Old-Timey Saloon Girls

SACRAMENTO WAS HOT and boring. Old Town's claim to fame seemed to be a splintery boardwalk crowded shoulder-to-shoulder with tourists searching for the saltwater taffy store.

It was a hundred and ten degrees outside. The heat made Rex sick to his stomach, and they couldn't leave the ferret and the dog in the Coach alone—they'd be fried—so Dad and Rex stayed with them, air conditioner running, in the parking structure.

Odette had suggested just skipping Old Town. She certainly wasn't interested. But Mom insisted. "This is the state capital, Odette!"

It was so hot on the boardwalk that Odette could smell the wooden planks practically baking in the sun, their scent wafting up on waves of heat. Beside her, Mom looked as wilted as Odette felt, and knowing she wasn't enjoying herself either gave Odette a grim sense of satisfaction.

"Want to go back?" Odette asked.

"No way!" Mom said. "We still haven't found that magic shop."

It was beyond unfair that while Rex got to lounge in the air conditioning, Odette was forced to tag along as Mom searched for a souvenir for him.

"He should have come with us if he wanted something," Odette said, even though she knew it was a waste of breath.

"Oh, Detters, you know how your brother gets in the heat," Mom said. She was scanning the shop signs, her attention only half on answering Odette. "He gets that terrible rash and his skin gets all itchy."

"I don't like it either," Odette said.

"Look!" Mom said. "There!"

She had found the store. At least it was cooler inside. Odette lurked near the door, trying to stay out of the way of the steady stream of tourists coming in and going out, and watched from a distance as her mother poked among the magic tricks.

After a while, Odette got tired of watching and wandered toward the back of the shop. There was one of those old-timey setups where you could dress like you were from the Old West and have a grainy sepia-toned photo taken.

"Do you want to take a picture?" the girl behind the counter asked.

"No," Odette said, but at the same time Mom came up and answered, "Definitely."

"No, Mom."

"Okay," said the girl. "Just pick an outfit. Take your time." She lifted up a section of the counter that was on hinges to let them through. Odette followed Mom.

"Let's be saloon girls." Mom headed right to the dresses after dropping a magic kit (The Magic of Science!) on the counter.

"None of those dresses will fit," Odette said. "I'll just wear a cowboy hat or something."

"I can make any dress fit," the girl said. Great, now she was in "helpful" mode.

"This one is fun." Mom plucked a purple satin gown from the rack and waved it at Odette.

Odette liked purple. A lot. She grudgingly took the dress.

"There's a great corset that goes with that one," said the girl. "I'll find it."

In the changing room—which was just the back corner of the store with a curtain drawn across it—Odette pulled off her shorts and T-shirt. She was glad she was wearing one of her three bras. When Mom had bought them for her six months ago, Rex had said, with his typical annoying honesty, "Aren't bras for girls with boobs?"

But that was six months ago. Now the bra felt sort of useful. And when Mom had packed the bathroom supplies in the Coach, she had shown Odette a corner of the cabinet where she'd tucked teen pads and tampons for when Odette had her "first moon," a euphemism that Odette thought was disgusting.

The purple dress was ridiculously big. "I don't think this fits," Odette said, sticking her head out of the curtain.

"No worries," said the girl, and she threw open the curtain. She was holding a black lace-up corset. "Turn around," she said.

Odette did, and she held out her arms as the girl cinched the extra purple fabric in the back and then laced up the corset on top of it. She pulled and adjusted and tied and then finally said, "There. Take a look."

There was a mirror just on the other side of the changing room. Odette blinked at her reflection. She liked the way she looked—the way the corset pulled her in at the middle, the flood of fabric around her ankles.

Mom appeared in the mirror behind her. "Detters," she said. "You look lovely."

Odette smiled, feeling silly and shy and happy all mixed together.

Mom didn't look bad either. She had the kind of boobs that corsets were made for, and the way they crested from the neckline of the dark green dress gave Odette hope for the future.

Then the girl arranged them by a big wine barrel in front of the cheesy saloon backdrop. She had Odette perch on top of it and positioned Odette's mom behind her. She backed up a few steps and peered through the camera. "Put your hand on her shoulder," she said to Mom. "You look like strangers."

Mom's warm palm pressed down on Odette's right shoulder. Odette felt each of her fingers, the hard ridge of her wedding ring. She felt for a moment like it was real—that she and Mom really were old-timey saloon girls, that they were a team, working together to make drinks and clean tables and do whatever else old-timey saloon girls did. Then the camera flashed and the girl said, "Got it," and Mom's hand lifted away.

Fish

AFTER SACRAMENTO, THEY cut across to the coast to escape the heat.

"This is way better than living in a house," Dad said. "If we don't like the weather, we can just go somewhere else!"

Odette didn't point out that at home the weather was never this miserably hot in the first place.

She had taped up the picture of her and Mom on the wall in her "room." Mom's head looked pretty funny in the big floppy hat she'd chosen, but they looked good together. Like a team. Odette wished she felt that way in real life.

It was markedly cooler on the coast. The road was tight and serpentine, and Dad drove the Coach extra slow, pulling to the side whenever someone wanted to pass. "No hurry, not a hurry in the world," he said, more to himself than anyone else. Odette sat buckled into the bench seat and watched the view—the soaring birds, the sharp-rocked cliffs, the low gray-tinged clouds drifting across the sky.

Rex sat across from her, riding backwards, which would have made Odette carsick. He stared out the window too, quiet for an unusually long time, as if hypnotized by the road unfurling behind them. Then, suddenly, his arm shot up. "What the heck is that!" he yelled. "Dad! Pull over! There's a fish in the road!"

They weren't going very fast anyway, and Dad drifted to a stop at the next turn-out.

"It must have been a dead squirrel," Mom said. "They get hit all the time."

"It was a fish," Rex said. "A big one. I'll show you."

"Okay," Dad said. "Let's go check it out." And Odette wasn't even surprised. That's how it went in their family.

When Rex wanted to park the Coach on the narrow shoulder of the skinny, windy road and go exploring, did her parents tell him he was insane? Of course not. They parked the Coach and everyone scrambled to follow him.

Odette left Georgie behind, and she made sure that the

Coach's door latched tightly. As annoying as the little dog was, Odette wouldn't want her to end up as roadkill.

"Hold hands!" Mom insisted.

They formed a chain, Dad in the front, then Rex, then Odette, with Mom bringing up the rear, and they laced their way back toward where Rex had seen the "fish," which Odette was certain was a squirrel. They were hundreds of feet above the ocean, which swirled and crashed down on the rocks below.

"There!" said Rex, yanking his hand away from Odette's and pointing.

"Well, I'll be damned," Dad said. "Look at that."

It was a fish. About a foot long, silver scaled, fantailed. In the middle of the highway.

"A bird must have dropped it," Mom said.

"I told you," Rex said. "I told you it was a fish." Now that he'd been proved right, he happily followed Mom's lead back to the Coach. But Odette kept looking back. The dead fish in the road seemed magical. Like an omen, or a curse.

Magic Lines

I DON'T KNOW," CAME Mieko's voice. "Not much, I guess. It's pretty boring here."

"Well, have you been going to the mall?" Odette was perched on the front steps of the Coach, the family cell phone pressed to her ear. It was a wonderful connection; Mieko sounded like she might have been sitting there beside her. They were camped in Crescent City, the northernmost coastal city in California. They had stayed three days while a local tire store ordered a replacement tire for the Coach and switched it back out for the spare. Today they would cross into Oregon.

Odette could hear the ocean from where she sat; it was foggy and cold, and she had her fleece jacket zipped all the way to the top.

"We've barely gone anywhere," Mieko said. "Mom's

been too busy. She says maybe we can do something this weekend."

Wasn't it the weekend? Odette found that she couldn't be exactly sure what day it was. Friday, maybe?

"What about you?" Mieko asked. "You're the one with all the excitement. Where are you guys?"

"Some campground," Odette said. "Today we'll go into Oregon. Rex is pretty excited about that."

"Because of Paul?"

"Uh-huh." It was funny—as soon as they crossed the invisible line between California and Oregon, Rex's ferret would stop being illegal contraband and would magically transform into a legitimate pet.

"Tell Rex I say congratulations," Mieko said, and then, "Listen, I've got to go. My sisters are fighting again." Mieko was the oldest of three girls, and their mom—who worked from home—paid Mieko during the summer to babysit.

It was funny how close Mieko had sounded on the phone but how far away she seemed as soon as they hung up. It was another of those magic lines, like the difference between California and Oregon—a phone connection.

Georgie, who had been waiting pretty patiently on Odette's lap while she talked to Mieko, looked up now and cocked her head as if to ask, *Walk time?*

"Sure, why not." Odette scooped the dog off her lap and set her on the ground.

Georgie shook herself, from her head all the way down to the tip of her skinny tail, and started off at a trot. Together they wandered up and down the rows of the tents and campers. Unlike that first campground in Buttonwillow, the Crescent City campground seemed to be doing a pretty steady business.

It was like a little temporary town, composed of blocks of RVs, trailers, and tents. And the inhabitants seemed like neighbors, the way they greeted each other in the misty morning air, nodding at Odette as she walked by with Georgie, as if they saw her every morning.

Odette led Georgie away from the campground and down toward the beach. The air was so thick with fog that the sandpipers by the water's edge looked like ghosts. Georgie's ears perked up. She growled and wagged her tail.

Except for Odette, Georgie, and the sandpipers, the

beach was empty. "Go for it," Odette said to Georgie, and she unclipped the leash from Georgie's harness.

The dog rocketed down the beach, spraying clumps of wet sand out behind her. For such a little dog, she sure was fast. The sandpipers ran and then lifted into the air when Georgie got close, settling a few feet down the beach and then lifting off again when she pursued them.

Odette played around too. She practiced her sprints, running away from the shoreline as the water washed in, then chasing the water back out when it receded. Again and again she ran from the water. Again and again she chased it back to sea. After a while, Georgie stopped stalking the sandpipers and plopped down on the sand, watching Odette run.

Finally Georgie barked and stood up, shaking the sand from her butt. She trotted down to the water's edge, right next to Odette, and when the next wave rolled in, she sprinted with Odette up the beach.

Odette laughed, delighted. "You funny little dog." She scooped Georgie up and rubbed the wet sand off her paws and chest. Georgie was shivering, either from cold or excitement, so Odette unzipped her fleece a little and tucked the dog inside.

A Long Way from Home

THEY OPENED ALL the windows as they approached the state line. Dad turned the radio way up—it didn't matter what song it was, just that it was loud and uptempo—and as they passed the sign that read WELCOME TO OREGON, Odette's parents and brother broke into cheers and laughter. Rex hoisted Paul, who had been sleeping in his lap, into the air. He pumped Paul's tiny ferret fist and yelled, "Freedom!"

Everyone laughed, even Odette, and with the cold fresh air hitting her face, with Rex's face so full of joy, with her parents' happiness so palpable, Odette felt happy too, and free, in spite of herself.

And then she turned and looked behind her, out the Coach's back window, across the highway. There, in the distance, was another sign, meant for the drivers heading the other way: WELCOME TO CALIFORNIA. And Odette watched that sign shrink and shrink until it disappeared.

Movie Night

THE FARTHER THEY drove through Oregon, the greener the world became. A quiet wet haze dampened every-thing. Not only were the roads wet, but sound seemed wet too. There was so much space here. So many grand ocean vistas, with white-capped gray waves and flocks of seabirds dive-bombing the ocean, hurtling themselves straight down into the water to reappear moments later, most times without a thing to show for their efforts, but every now and then one would resurface with a juicy fish pinched in its beak.

They camped for two days in Yachats, which looked like "Ya-cats," but actually was pronounced "Ya-hats." Here, unlike back home, giant pine trees meandered down hillsides, disappearing only for the width of the highway before reappearing on the other side of the road, wandering all the way down to the sand as if they fancied a day at the seaside. And their pine needles didn't look dry and forest-firey the way they did in the mountains back home. Here they looked bendy and soft, like dark green porcupine quills.

They took a detour midway up the Oregon coast, veering inland across Highway 20, to visit Mom's old college town. They ate a pizza that was, admittedly, better than any pizza Odette had ever eaten back home. Driving out of town, down a country road, they passed a tall yellow two-story house. A wind turbine spun lazily behind it and Odette saw a family — a man, a woman, and a girl about her age — working in the garden. The blue sky was open like a trusting face.

In Astoria, way up at the top of Oregon, they camped for a full week. It was a KOA campground, which stood for "Kampgrounds of America," purposefully misspelled. This irritated Rex so much that he could barely stand to stay there, even with the "Bounce Pillow," a giant air-filled red and yellow dome that kids jumped on for hours.

There was a pool, too, an indoor one because of all the rain. Steamy twice-breathed air filled the pool house, and the happy screams of little kids reverberated off the walls.

Rex splashed and swam until he grew pruney, wax

plugs jammed into his ears to soften the noise of all the people, nose plugs clamped over his nostrils to keep out the water.

The last night at the Astoria campground, Odette's parents insisted they watch this old movie called *The Goonies*. The four of them — plus Georgie — smashed together side by side on the big bed at the back of the Coach. Mom's lap held the popcorn. The movie was about this group of misfit kids who lived in Astoria, Oregon. Their homes were threatened by rich bad guys who wanted to tear them down to build a golf course. The kids found a treasure map and headed off on an adventure of epic proportions. In the end, the kids find the treasure and save their neighborhood.

Odette knew her parents thought it would be fun to watch *The Goonies* because it was set in Astoria and they were actually in Astoria. But she could tell from the look on Dad's face when the movie began that he'd forgotten about the whole losing-their-home element of the story.

It

IT WAS DISGUSTING.

She knew what they were doing, and she couldn't *believe* they were doing it. Here. In the Coach. With only, like, thirty feet between their bed and hers. With Rex asleep on the fold-out bed.

Odette knew her parents thought she was asleep too, or there was *no way* they'd be doing that—making out or having sex or whatever it was they were doing exactly. They had closed the ridiculous privacy curtain; maybe that was what had woken her—the raspy sound of the divider being pulled shut.

Or maybe it was their whispered laughter. Whatever had woken her, and whatever they were doing, it was disgusting.

"I can hear you," she said. "I'm awake up here."

Silence. Sudden, satisfying silence.

Then her mom said, still from behind the curtain, "Oh, Detters, we're just talking. Go back to sleep, honey."

"Sure you are," Odette muttered. She rolled over onto her side and pulled her pillow up over her ear.

Uno

THE CAMPGROUND IN Washington was nothing like the KOA campground in Astoria. That one had been like an amusement park compared to this place. Here, there was no "Year-Round Heated Pool!," no "Giant Bounce Pillow!," no mini golf, no campwide sing-alongs or marshmallow roasts or snack bar or wifi or *anything*. Here there were just trees.

That expression about not being able to see the forest for the trees made perfect sense here. Odette felt that the trees crowded out the light, sky—everything.

And there was something wrong with the Coach's waste line, which meant they couldn't use the toilet or shower until they got to Seattle, where they could buy a replacement part.

"It won't be so bad," Dad said. "We're camped close to the bathhouse. And the showers take quarters!"

She didn't see how that was a good thing.

Rex thought it was cool, though. "It's like a game," he said, "to see if you can get your whole body washed and rinsed before the water runs out."

"You can take two quarters, you know," Odette said.

"Where's the challenge in that?"

One thing the trees did not keep out was rain. Almost immediately after they'd leveled the Coach and hooked up the electricity, it began to pour.

Dad rushed back inside and slammed the door behind him.

"Well, let's hope I plugged everything in right," he said. "It'd be a shame to turn the Coach into a giant toaster, and us into the toast."

Everyone laughed at that, except Odette. What was *wrong* with these people? There was nothing funny about accidental electrocution. There was nothing funny about being stuck in this stupid storm, the rain pelting the metal roof of the Coach in a cacophony of misery.

Rex let Paul out of the bathroom so he could wander around for a while. Georgie watched from Odette's lap as the ferret found a few crumbs in the kitchenette and then disappeared.

"Who wants to play Uno?" Mom asked.

Uno had to be the dumbest game invented. Ever.

"I'll play, I guess," Odette said. What else was she going to do? They all squeezed around the tiny table, Mom and Rex sliding into the bench on one side and Dad and Odette on the other. Mom shuffled the cards and passed them around. Three times cards slid off the end of the table. It just wasn't big enough. The third time, Odette didn't retrieve the card and pretended not to notice when Georgie snatched it and took it to the back of the Coach to shred it. It was a good card, too. A Draw Four Wild.

Rex was like an Uno savant. He won, as he almost always did. The Coach felt steamy with all their bodies pressed together around the table. The walls around them seemed to shrink toward one another, and Odette's throat constricted too.

"I've gotta get out of here," she said, getting up and shrugging into her raincoat.

"Take the dog," her mom called after her.

Outside, even though it was raining crazy hard, at least she could *breathe.* Georgie, pulling on the harness, seemed amped up by the rain. Her ears flattened against her head, her eyes narrowed into slits. Odette didn't care where they went, so she just let Georgie lead the way.

The dog scrunched up into her poop squat under an enormous pine tree, and when she was done, Odette just kicked some wet pine needles over it. Georgie sniffed the pile in that gross way dogs do. Then, even though she was dreading going back inside, Odette couldn't think of anything else to do but head back toward the Coach.

"Detters!" Mom appeared on the path, her hair flattened by the rain. She wasn't wearing her raincoat. "Honey, have you seen Paul?"

"What?"

"Paul," Mom said, sounding desperate. "He got out."

"You didn't close the door," Rex wailed. He didn't even have on shoes. "You let him escape."

"I shut the door," Odette argued, but with a sick feeling in her stomach that maybe she didn't. She couldn't remember hearing it latch.

"It doesn't matter," Mom said. "We just need to find Paul."

"Paul! Paul!" Dad shone a flashlight at the base of a tree just next to the Coach. "Come on, Paul."

They spread out, eyes on the ground, the rain coming

down in unrelenting sheets. Odette blinked the raindrops from her eyes, scanning the earth around her for any sign of movement, for a flash of Paul's white weasel body. Nothing. Just pine needles and rain all around.

Georgie seemed to get that they were looking for something. Her ears perked up into alert and her nose snarfed along. At first Odette envisioned Georgie revealing herself as a hero dog, upturning a pile of pine needles to uncover Paul. But no. Georgie snuffled around aimlessly.

They searched until they were soaked through; they searched until it was dark. They searched until, at last, Dad scooped up Rex's unwilling, crying body and carried him back to the Coach.

"Paul's probably just hunkered down somewhere waiting out the storm," Dad said. He stripped Rex down to his dinosaur-patterned boxer shorts in the kitchenette and rubbed him all over with a towel. Rex's fingers were blue. His nose was running.

"He's all alone out there," Rex wailed. "He thinks I've abandoned him!"

"No, no," soothed Mom. She stood and dripped, petting Rex's hair. "Paul could never think that," she said. "Paul knows how much you love him."

It was awful. And it was all Odette's fault.

Mom found Rex's favorite pajamas, and Dad fixed him a mug of hot chocolate, and Odette did her best to stay out of the way, drying off Georgie and stripping out of her heavy wet clothes in the tiny little bathroom. She threw her wet things into the shower and then took Georgie up to bed. Her stomach rumbled in hungry disappointment, but she just wanted to disappear.

When she got under the covers, she felt something down by her feet. Warm, and fuzzy, and alive. "Paul!" she said. She fished under the blankets and came out with a bleary-eyed sleepy ferret. "It's Paul!"

"Thank god," Dad said, and Mom cheered, and Rex clambered up the ladder to snatch the ferret from Odette's hands.

"You bad boy," he crooned, snuggling Paul close and kissing him again and again before taking him back down. "I didn't know you could climb a ladder!"

Absolutely ridiculous. "I can't believe you guys didn't look for him," Odette said. She was furious.

"Detters, honey, of course we looked for him! Just not up there."

Honestly, Mom could be *so* oblivious. "I don't get it,"

Odette said. "Why do you guys immediately have to jump all the way to crazy? You should look *everywhere* before making us all trudge around in the rain. Don't you know how to do *anything*?"

They all looked up at her, even Paul with his beady little red eyes. At last Dad said, "Honey, this isn't really about the ferret, is it?"

She would cry if she spoke. Either that, or she would scream. Again, the walls seemed to grow closer, the air to thicken. Without a word, Odette pulled the covers up over her head.

Footpath

THE MORNING AFTER the rain, Odette went for a run. She took Georgie for a short walk first, and then deposited her back into the Coach before double-knotting the laces of her running shoes and heading back out. Odette's breath preceded her like a little cloud as she picked up a jog just outside the Coach.

The campground consisted of a dozen or so inlets carved into the forest, each with an RV or trailer parked in it. They'd had to clear trees to make room for parking and to build the road that wound down the middle of the campground. Everywhere else the trees grew thick like hair.

All of the RVs sat still and dark; when Odette passed the farthest one, which bore a little sign reading CAMP HOST, and curved onto a stretch of the asphalt road that led out toward the main highway, she picked up her pace, lengthening her stride.

Mom had told her to stay off the main road, but a walking path ran alongside the highway, slightly lower than the road, carpeted by pine needles.

The path, soaked from last night's rain, absorbed Odette's footfalls. As tight and trapped as she had felt last night, that was exactly how free she felt now, breathing in the sharp, cold early-morning air, her muscles unwinding as they warmed. She could outrun anything right now, that was how strong she felt.

Cute Boy in Line
to Buy Food

I SN'T IT FUNNY," said Rex, "that we're in a house that's a car on a boat?"

They stopped in Seattle and then drove north to Anacortes, Washington, where they waited four hours to board the ferry that would take them to Orcas Island. Mom had made the ferry reservations before they'd even left California; to transport something as big and heavy as the Coach, the ferry required advance notice.

After some low-level cursing as he maneuvered the Coach onto the ferry and into its parking spot on the bottom level, Dad cut the engine. They sat listening to the quiet ticking Odette had grown used to in the three weeks since the Coach had become her home until Mom said, "Well, let's go see the ferry!"

Georgie had peed before they'd boarded, so Odette left her sleeping on the big bed. Dad locked the door behind them, and even though they were squished between a bunch of cars in a floating parking lot, it felt oddly like back home, when they'd leave for the day and Dad would lock up on their way out.

The ferryboat was huge. It was called the *Yakima,* and it was white with green stripes along the sides. From the dock Odette had seen its rows and rows of windows stacked three high. Now, on the lowest level, she followed Dad to the far back of the boat — the stern, he'd said it was called — and up a set of metal stairs that reminded her of the Coach's stairs.

They emerged in the galley to find themselves among a crowd of tourists taking their seats on benches along the windows. A line formed in front of the snack bar, where two harried-looking servers rang up orders of coffee and candy bars.

There was a boy in line for snacks. Actually, there were lots of boys in line for snacks, but this one gave Odette the tingly-anticipation feeling she got just before running.

He had earbuds in, and he wasn't *dancing,* exactly, but his whole body sort of vibrated with whatever music he was listening to. He was wearing all black — black T-shirt, black jeans, black Chuck Taylors — in a way that normally

Odette would roll her eyes at, but on him it seemed to make sense. He was dark everywhere else, too—dark skin, dark hair, dark eyes—and he wore his hair short on the sides, with a longer strip down the middle, which he kept running his hand over.

"Mom," Odette said, "give me the phone, okay?"

Mom had been digging through her purse already, looking for money to give to Rex, who wanted a cup of hot chocolate, so she found the phone almost immediately, which was nice for a change. More often than not, it seemed, the family cell phone was lost at the bottom of her immense bag, its battery completely drained.

This time it was at almost full charge. Odette did her best impression of a spy as she held up the phone to take a picture of the boy, pretending that she was super interested in the sign just behind his head.

Then she sent the picture to Mieko.

Almost immediately the phone pinged back. *Cute! Who is he? Where r u?*

Stinging tears filled Odette's eyes. They were tears of relief, and they surprised her. Mieko had been harder to get ahold of the last week or so, but Odette told herself that she understood. Between babysitting her sisters and hanging out with her other friends back home, of course Mieko was busy. She couldn't be expected to always answer when Odette called, or respond to every text.

And Odette had been pulling back too, because she didn't want to seem needy or anything. But a boy—that was something the two of them could talk about for a while. Mieko wasn't exactly boy crazy, but she was, of the two of them, way more likely to notice a guy.

On a boat, Odette typed. *Cute boy in line to buy food.*

"Hey."

The voice interrupted Odette before she could hit Send. She looked up. The boy from the snack line stood directly in front of her, holding a bag of potato chips and a soda can.

"Did you take my picture?"

If a zombie had appeared in that moment, wandering through the galley searching for brains, Odette would have gladly offered hers.

"Um," she said.

"Do I know you?" The boy didn't look mad. Confused, maybe, or embarrassed.

"No," she managed to say.

"No, you didn't take my picture?"

"No, I did take your picture," Odette said. "I meant, no, you don't know me. I'm sorry," she said, shoving the phone in her pocket.

"It's the hair, isn't it?" he said. "It looks ridiculous."

The boy looked miserable, and this time when he ran his hand through his hair, Odette realized that he was embarrassed about it. "No, your hair is cool," she said. She couldn't believe she was standing here talking to this guy about his hair.

He didn't look like he believed her, and Odette figured, what the heck, she'd never see him again anyway, so she pulled out her phone and thrust it in his direction. "Here," she said. She watched his eyes widen as he thumbed through the texts between her and Mieko, and a grin spread across his face.

"Cool," he said, handing back the phone.

It was maybe the most awkward Odette had ever felt. But it was worth it — the relief in the boy's face, the open smile.

"I'm Harris," he said.

"Hi," said Odette. "I'm Odette."

"Detters," said Odette's mom, right behind her suddenly. "We're going up to the sun deck to look for dolphins. Come on!"

Harris smirked a little, probably because of her embarrassing nickname.

"Sure," said Odette, and then, in a jolt of bravery, to Harris, "Wanna come?"

"Okay," he said.

Dolphin Pod

THEY MADE THEIR way through the galley and up another flight of stairs, Odette keenly aware of Harris right behind her. When they emerged on the sun deck, Odette couldn't help but take a deep, gulping breath of the damp salty air.

This was, Odette thought as she leaned against the dark wood railing, watching the foam of waves against the side of the ferry, the closest she had ever come to a date. She couldn't have been more nervous if a horde of zombies rounded the corner in her direction.

Harris leaned against the rail next to her, his arm so close that she could feel the fabric of his jacket brushing against her fleece. She stole a sideways glance. Tapping fingers, shock-wide eyes. He looked as bad as she felt. At least that was something.

Then, "Boats make me sick," he said.

"Oh." Odette didn't know what to say to that. "Maybe chips and soda weren't the best idea?"

"Yeah. I thought eating a snack might distract me, but I guess not." He grinned and looked at Odette. "Maybe you can distract me," he said, which Odette resolved to remember exactly so she could report it later to Mieko.

"Um," she said.

"Are you guys on vacation?"

"Sort of," Odette said.

"How can you be 'sort of' on vacation?"

"It's kind of complicated." The boat lurched to the left, and they both grabbed on to the rail to keep their balance.

Harris took a deep, slow breath through his nose, like he was trying to keep from puking.

He really *did* need to be distracted. "We lived in Southern California until a few weeks ago," Odette blurted. The words poured out of her easily now. "My dad lost his job, and my Grandma Sissy has been sick, so my parents decided this would be a good time to take a break from everything and go on an adventure."

Her story seemed to have done the trick, or maybe the

boat's motion had mellowed. Either way, Harris seemed less ill. "No way," he said.

"Yes way," Odette answered. "That's why we're going to Orcas Island. That's where Grandma Sissy lives." A moment passed, uncomfortable, both of them silent. Then Odette blurted, "What about you?"

"Mom and I are on vacation. We're going to spend a week touring the islands. Orcas first, and then Fidalgo."

"Cool," said Odette. She couldn't think of a follow-up question. The silence between them condensed like the clouds overhead.

"Hey," said Harris. He smiled widely and pointed out into the blue-gray sea. "You think those are dolphins?"

Odette narrowed her eyes and scanned the water. She didn't see anything at first, but then—there! A fin, and then another, and then three more.

"It's a pod! A pod!" Rex ran across the sun deck, his arms flailing wildly as he lost his balance and skidded from side to side before ramming into Harris. "Look!"

"We see them, Rex," said Odette.

Rex shoved himself in between Harris and Odette at the rail. He bounced up on the balls of his feet in his Rex way and pulled the neck of his T-shirt into his mouth so he could suck on it, which he did when he got excited or nervous. Half his shirts had gross stretched-out neckbands. Odette shot a look at Harris to see if he was weirded out by Rex, but he didn't seem to notice, his eyes focused out to sea. Together they watched the dolphins swim at an angle toward the ferry. All along the boat's edge, people lined up to see the pod. When they got close to the boat—just a few feet from it—the dolphins swam right alongside it, as if they were playing around.

Everyone pulled out their cameras and cell phones, recording the dolphins or taking pictures. A youngish dad held his daughter up so she could see, and she waved her chubby little hand like she was saying hello.

Behind them, in the center of the sun deck, a couple of guys and a girl in stripey tall socks pulled out some instruments—a banjo and a fiddle and a harmonica—and they started playing a jaunty song.

The dolphins swam with the boat like they had nowhere else they needed to be, nothing else they needed to do. The music floated like a happy balloon. Odette felt, right then, like the dolphins, like the music. Free.

Furies

MAYBE WE COULD meet up on the island," Harris suggested, sort of shy. "We'll be on Orcas for three days."

"That would be fun," said Odette, trying not to look too excited. "I could give you my number if you want." Then, embarrassed, "We all share one phone. It's a long, annoying story, but if you put my name in the text, my parents will let me know."

"Cool," said Harris, and they both pulled out their phones. Enviously, Odette noted that his phone was personalized, with a purple and black skull sticker on the back.

Just ahead, Orcas Island appeared out of the misty sky—bigger than she'd expected it to be, with wide double humps and an uneven curved shoreline that bent inward on itself like a horseshoe. A flock of black birds carved loose circles high up in the sky.

"Well," said Harris, "see ya." He turned abruptly and walked away. Odette watched him go. He walked with one shoulder—his left—slightly higher than the other.

"He seemed nice," Mom said, and Odette could tell that she'd been waiting a few steps away, trying to give Odette her space.

"Uh-huh." Odette knew her mom wanted her to say more than that—she could tell by the way her mom just stood there, smiling a little, waiting—but she didn't feel like saying anything, so she turned around and headed toward the stairs.

It was taking a while for the ferry to dock, and it would be at least another half an hour before it would be their turn to drive the Coach onto the shore. Georgie looked like she needed to pee again, so Odette laid down one of the "puddle pads" they had in case of emergencies, but instead of peeing on it, the dog flopped down and started chewing a corner.

Rex was looking for something. He dug through his

plastic tote, making a mess with all his toys, and then he slammed through a bunch of cabinets, even the ones in the kitchenette. His features were converging into a dangerous potential storm.

"Mom," he said, finally.

She was sitting in the captain's chair, reading a book. "Mm-hm," she said.

"I can't find my Whales, Porpoises, and Dolphins Cube," he said. "Do you know where it is?"

Mom shut her book. "Oh, honey," she said. "You sold it at the yard sale, remember?"

Rex shook his head, hard. "No," he said. "I didn't. I sold some of the other Cubes, but I would never sell *that* one."

Uh-oh.

"Honey," Mom said again, using her sweetest voice, the one she used when she was trying to head off one of Rex's furies. "You did sell it. Remember? With all the other Cubes. For thirty-five dollars."

"I didn't," wailed Rex. "I wouldn't!"

He would and he did. Odette remembered, but she knew better than to get involved. It had been a long time since Rex had had a fury, but Odette recognized the signs.

His fists clenching and unclenching. His face reddening. His eyes blinking way too much.

And Georgie—though she'd never been around for one of Rex's furies—seemed nervous too. She'd stopped gnawing on the corner of the puddle pad and was sitting very still, her ears pressed tight against the sides of her head. She whined a little.

Odette scooped her up and headed to the front of the Coach. Dad wasn't back yet—"Taking advantage of the full-size toilet" is how he put it—and Odette knew from experience that she would just be in the way if Rex really got going. She put Georgie on her bed and climbed up too.

"I want my Cube!" Rex's voice rose and rose. "You sold my Cube!"

Mom spoke to him in her special soothing voice. She was doing that thing that was supposed to calm Rex down, squeezing his arms gently and consistently.

"I hate this!" Rex screamed. "I can't believe you made me sell all my stuff! I can't believe you sold our house! You ruined everything!"

Usually when Rex had a fury, it made Odette mad. His furies sucked all of the family's attention into them, all of their energy. By the time he recovered, everyone felt like they'd had the stomach flu. Worn out, stripped down, empty.

But this time, she pretty much agreed with him.

Then Rex started the scream-cry-laugh thing he did. He didn't hit Mom anymore, the way he did when he was really little. He hit himself, instead, which seemed just as awful, pounding his fists against his thighs, which made Mom even more upset than if he'd hit *her*.

"You're going to hurt yourself," she said, trying to restrain him, but Rex had gotten strong and he kept pounding his legs.

"I want my Cube!"

"We can get another one," Mom promised. "We can order one online."

In that moment, if Rex had wanted his own cell phone, Odette knew her mother's only question would have been which model.

"I don't want another one," Rex cried. "I want *my* one." But he was crying and breathing weird, and so his words didn't come out clean.

Mom started crying too, and she pulled Rex close. "I

know," she said. She rocked him back and forth, back and forth.

Odette tucked Georgie's head underneath her chin, holding her tight, letting the dog lick her neck. Her own tears dripped onto Georgie's black fur.

The Coach's door rattled open. "Hey ho, what's all this?" said Dad, standing in the doorway.

His arrival didn't help. When Mom saw him, she cried harder, and Rex did too, and Odette did her very best to shrink and disappear, taking Georgie with her.

The Dutch Door

B Y THE TIME they finally drove the Coach off the ferry, Rex had exhausted himself. He slept in a tight little ball on the back bed, Paul curled up beside him.

Everyone else was exhausted too. It was completely unfair. Odette knew that her brother would awake from his nap refreshed and happy, as if his fury had pressed an invisible reset button. But the rest of them—Mom, Dad, Odette—would be drained for the remainder of the day. Odette's eyes would feel swollen and tired, as if she'd been the one who'd had the terrible tantrum. Her parents would get all quiet and soft, and even though they rarely drank alcohol, they'd both want a glass of wine later, after Rex had gone to sleep for the night.

After a fury, there was no way to tell how long the reset would last. Rex could have another fury the next day, or it could be weeks. Maybe that was the worst part, worse than the fury itself—the anticipation, the not-knowing.

THE SKY WAS bright with sunset as Mom drove the Coach away from the dock and toward Grandma Sissy's house. Odette focused on being right there, on that road, seeing everything and thinking about nothing else. She had only been to Orcas Island once before in her life, when her mom was pregnant with Rex. Odette had been four years old and her only memories of Orcas Island were the warm, tangy smell of the bread Grandma Sissy baked each morning in her shop and the leathery black-and-white of an orca itself, though she might be merging another memory, from Sea World, now that she thought about it. The bread, maybe, was all she had left.

Usually Grandma Sissy was the one to visit them. "One plane ticket rather than four" was what Dad said about it. But a couple of years ago, when Grandma Sissy had been diagnosed with breast cancer and had to have surgery, Mom had gone up alone to take care of her.

Since then, after she recovered, Grandma Sissy had visited them twice, and they talked on the phone every few weeks, but it had been a year since Odette had seen her at all.

Odette had expected that returning to Orcas Island would feel like walking through a dream, that she'd see things she hadn't exactly remembered but that felt familiar. As they drove from the ferry dock into Eastsound Village, though, she recognized nothing. Not the high-roofed shingled buildings, not the inviting white front porches, not the near-empty streets, the missing stoplights. None of it.

At last Mom pulled the Coach over to the side of the road, thrusting the gearshift into park. She raised her chin at a building on the corner. "There." She looked over her shoulder at Odette. "Now, Detters, remember, Grandma Sissy has been sick . . ."

Odette barely heard her. She was staring out the window at Grandma Sissy's bakery. A hand-lettered red and white sign read SISSY'S BREADS AND SWEETS. The lights on the bottom floor were out, but upstairs—where Grandma Sissy lived—every room glowed brightly.

Odette didn't wait for her parents to wake up Rex. She didn't take Georgie with her, even though the dog must have really, really needed to pee after the ferry ride. She just banged through the Coach's door and raced across the sidewalk, overwhelmed suddenly with excitement at the thought of being in a real house again, with doors and full-size toilets.

"Grandma Sissy!" she called up at the open, glowing window. "We're here!"

"I can see that," came Grandma Sissy's voice—and that *was* familiar. "I'll be right down."

Odette heard her family coming out of the Coach to join her, she heard Dad reprimand her—"Odette, your poor dog practically wet herself"—she heard the clinking of Mom's keys. But she didn't look at any of them. She looked at the bakery's friendly door—a gray-blue Dutch door, shut now, and a tiny spark of memory recalled it, how the top could swing loose while the bottom stayed shut, the cheery jingle of the bell fastened to its handle inside.

It jingled just then, exactly as Odette suddenly anticipated it would. And then the door swung open. And there, on its other side, with Grandma Sissy's smile, stood a stranger.

Does Anybody Want a Cookie?

T *WAS* GRANDMA Sissy, Odette determined. There
was her smile, and her dark brown eyes, and the same
long gray-white hair—the longest of any grandmother
Odette knew. And she was wearing the necklace she
always wore, a round gold medallion on a gold chain.

It was that everything else looked different. Her
stomach jutted out like a pregnant lady's, and the rest
of her—her face, her chest, her arms—was so skinny,
almost skeletal. She leaned her weight on a cane that
she held in her right hand, as if just standing upright was
exhausting her.

Behind her, Odette heard Mom's cheery greeting fail
on her lips and transform from a "Hello!" to "Oh my god."
She heard Dad say, "Oh, Sissy."

Grandma Sissy's smile faltered. "It's that obvious, is it?"

For a moment, no one said a word.

Finally Grandma Sissy said, "It's so good to see you all," and then she stepped back into the shop to make room for them. "Don't just stand there on the street," she said. "Come inside!"

Inside smelled like memory. Warm baked bread. Cinnamon. Vanilla. A marble counter topped the glass-fronted display cases, which in the morning would be filled with bread and cakes and cookies. Butterscotch walls and silver light fixtures made the whole shop glow. It looked like the homiest place in the world.

"Does anybody want a cookie?" Grandma Sissy asked as they passed a red ceramic jar on the display case. No one did but Rex. Grandma Sissy got him a snickerdoodle and then they all followed her upstairs.

It was even nicer up there, and with a rush of sadness Odette missed her own home all over again: end tables with lamps that weren't attached to them. Pictures on the walls. Full-size furniture.

Odette looked very carefully at a painting that hung above the couch. It was an ocean scene with a blue sky, white clouds, and birds dipping down toward the water.

She took a step closer and looked at the texture of the paint, the ripples where the blue-gray sea peaked into waves, the careful feathering of birds' wings. She tried as hard as she could to focus on what was in front of her and ignore, just for a minute or two, what she knew was behind her—Grandma Sissy, and her mom's tear-drippy face, and her dad's shocked expression. She blinked away blurry tears and stared at one particular dollop of white paint in the lower left corner of the painting, a swirly twist in the water.

"Odette," Mom said. "You and Rex go get ready for bed, okay?"

She could have argued that it wasn't all that late, that they just got here, that Georgie needed a long walk before bed. But she didn't.

"The smaller guest room is all set up for you and Rex," Grandma Sissy said. "Right at the end of the hall." She hugged Rex and kissed the top of his head, and then it was Odette's turn. When Grandma Sissy's arms went around her, Odette closed her eyes to pretend that nothing was different, but even with her eyes closed she could feel the hard lump of Grandma Sissy's belly; she could smell medicine, or something like that that didn't smell very good at all. Not like the bakery downstairs, the way Grandma Sissy used to smell.

"We'll visit in the morning," Grandma Sissy said.

Dad said, "C'mon, guys, I'll help you get settled in," and he put one hand on Odette's shoulder and the other on Rex's, and steered them down the hall.

What Are the Odds?

REX WAS SLEEPING, and so was Georgie. Odette was tucked into bed too, but she was wide awake. The walls around her felt solid and reliable. The pillows were thick and downy. And Odette, luxuriating in the feeling of soft sheets and a real mattress beneath her, felt like the world's worst human being for enjoying any of it.

The house was old, and it had brass slatted heating vents on the floor, one right near Odette's bed and another, she surmised, in her parents' room, because if she was careful to breathe quietly, she could hear their conversation.

"She looks terrible," Mom said. "Just terrible."

"Her body looks pretty worn down," Dad said, "but her attitude seems really good."

"Her *attitude* won't keep her alive, Simon."

"I know. I know that."

Then there was the sound of Mom crying — messy, sad crying, not the happy kind like at school recitals and on Mother's Day after she opened her cards. But it was muffled, like she had her face in a pillow or against Dad's shirt. She probably didn't want any of them to hear her — not Odette or Rex and certainly not Grandma Sissy.

"What are the odds?" Dad said. "Who recovers from breast cancer and then gets appendiceal cancer?"

"It doesn't matter what the odds are," Mom said.

"Of course not," Dad said. "I know."

Then Odette didn't want to hear anymore — about cancer, or odds, or anything. She flipped onto her side, pulled the pillow over her head, and pressed it hard against her ear. Appendiceal cancer. What did that even mean?

It sounded kind of like *appendix,* which Odette knew was a body part, but she didn't know what it was for or even where it was, exactly. Somewhere near the stomach.

And cancer — she didn't know much about that, either. She knew Grandma Sissy had had it, and now that she had long crescent scars where her breasts had been. Odette had seen them once, accidentally, when Grandma Sissy had been getting out of the shower the last time she visited. It wasn't Odette's fault — Grandma Sissy hadn't locked the door—and she'd felt really bad how scared it made her feel and how ugly the scars were. But after Grandma Sissy was dressed, she'd come into Odette's room and then it was all right again. She looked like herself once her clothes were on.

This was different. Clothes couldn't hide what was wrong with Grandma Sissy this time. Nothing could.

Morning

ODETTE SMELLED THE warm yeasty scent of baking bread before she even opened her eyes. She lay very still and breathed as deeply as she could, over and over. She heard rain hitting the roof and she smelled bread and she saw nothing.

But Georgie must have sensed that she was awake, because the little dog whined her special "It's time to wake up and go outside" whine, and for what felt like the hundredth time, Odette wondered what in the heck her dad was thinking when he brought home this runty little mutt. But, just behind that thought was another, one that she'd thought close to ninety-nine times . . . She was glad he did.

Then Odette opened her eyes. The sky outside the window had barely begun to glow with daylight, and filtered by the rain, it looked pretty dreary. She sat up and stretched, tucking Georgie under her arm before she stood. Rex was still sleeping on the pull-out trundle bed on the floor, Paul in a small cage by his feet, so Odette scooted carefully around him and closed the door behind her.

It was weird to be staying in a real house again, with doors and furniture. It was weird not to have her whole family within the line of her sight at the same time. Not bad weird. Not good weird either. Just . . . weird.

Grandma Sissy's house was quiet except for the deep, steady breathing—and occasional snore—from Dad just next door. She couldn't hear Mom, but Mom was a quiet breather, so there was no way to know without looking if Mom was still in bed or if she was downstairs with Grandma Sissy.

Odette's stomach felt churny and uneasy. Like a roller coaster might make it feel, but without the excitement, just the dread. Sort of afraid, like maybe it wasn't just her grandmother down there in the kitchen, getting her shop ready for the day's customers. Like maybe it was something else—something part grandmother and part not-grandmother.

Odette debated sneaking back into bed for another hour or so, until she was sure at least one of her parents was awake. But Georgie wiggled around in her arms, reminding Odette that she *had* to go outside if she didn't want dog pee all over herself. So she clipped Georgie's leash onto her harness, found her jacket and boots near the staircase, and headed down to the shop below.

It looked almost exactly as it had looked the night before, except this morning gray light streamed in through the big front windows. Odette heard Grandma Sissy moving around in the back, where the ovens were, but Georgie's excitement over going outside gave her a good reason not to go back there and say good morning.

She forgot about the bell hanging from the handle until it was too late, and she cringed as it jangled, but then she set Georgie down on the sidewalk and followed her lead.

The rain was misty now, but cold, as if the ocean were in the air. Odette kept her head down and her free hand tucked into her pocket. Georgie seemed surprised by the cold too, and in a hurry to get back inside. She peed almost right away, just a couple of buildings up, underneath a tree. Odette looked away while the dog peed; it seemed rude to stare. Instead she looked into the shop they were in front of. It was a bookstore, and she thought maybe she could come back when it was open and look for something new to read. She could see that they had a small toy collection in the back and wondered briefly if they might stock animal Cubes. Wouldn't that be amazing if they had a Whales, Porpoises, and Dolphins one? She would be a hero if she brought one of those back for Rex.

Then the rain started to come down harder and the prospect of facing Grandma Sissy began to seem better than being outside, so Odette said, "Come on, Georgie, let's go back," and the dog seemed to agree that was a good idea, because she followed right along and didn't pull on the leash the way she sometimes did.

As Odette pushed open the door to go back into the bakery, the sun finished rising behind her. Though the day was still wet and gray, the sky brightened. Odette felt terribly hungry, and she wondered if maybe she could get one of those cookies before everyone else woke up.

Breakfast Tray

IT TURNED OUT that it wasn't Grandma Sissy in the kitchen. It was another lady, someone Odette didn't recognize. When Odette came back inside, shedding her boots and jacket near the door, she headed for the kitchen to find something to dry Georgie with. A tall, broad-shouldered woman with hair more gunmetal gray than silver worked over a well-floured counter, rolling out dough.

She was old, for sure—as she leaned forward over her work, the skin of her neck and arms rolled forward too, as if she was made of muscular dough. She didn't look fragile like Grandma Sissy had the night before—in fact, seeing this woman made Odette twinge with extra sadness about Grandma Sissy, who seemed like a wispy reed in contrast.

The lady looked up and smiled. "You must be Odette,"

she said. "I'd shake your hand, but . . ." She waggled her flour-covered fingers. "I'm Bea," she said. "Sissy's friend."

"Hello," said Odette. "This is Georgie." She waved one of Georgie's front paws.

Bea smiled. "That sure is a cute little mutt," she said. "Just make sure to stash her in the flour barrel if the health department stops by." Then she winked to show she was joking. "Want a morning bun? Fresh from the oven."

Odette nodded and slid onto a red metal stool across the counter from Bea. There was a hand towel on the counter that wasn't too flour-dusted, and when Bea turned away to slip a bun onto a plate, Odette snuck the towel and rubbed Georgie dry.

"Is Grandma Sissy still sleeping?"

"She's usually awake by now, but resting. Do you want to bring her a breakfast tray?"

Odette shrugged, then nodded. She ate her bun and watched Bea assemble a tray in what looked to be a practiced fashion—pouring hot water from a kettle over tea leaves, filling a little pitcher with cream, putting a morning bun and a cut-up apple on a plate, and finally, filling a little white ramekin with a rainbow of pills.

"Is Grandma Sissy dying?" Odette blurted. It was seeing all those pills that made her ask.

Bea looked at Odette like she was sizing her up. Her weight leaned on one leg, her hands flat on the counter in front of her. She said, "Not one of us lives forever, honey. Why don't you take this tray up to your grandma?"

Odette nodded, though she felt like saying no. "Will you watch Georgie?"

"It'll be an honor," Bea said. "Does your dog like bacon, by any chance?"

AT THE TOP of the stairs, Odette balanced the tray in one hand while she knocked softly on Grandma Sissy's door with the other.

"Come in," called Grandma Sissy's voice, and again there was that feeling like everything was just fine. Odette twisted the doorknob and pushed open the door. Grandma Sissy was in bed, but she was sitting up with a bunch of pillows behind her. Curtains kept the room dark except for a circle of yellow light cast by the lamp at her bedside.

Grandma Sissy was reading. She looked up from her

book and smiled. Her glasses perched crookedly on her nose. When she pulled them off, they dangled from a beaded chain around her neck.

"Good morning, my darling!" she said. "You brought me breakfast."

"Bea fixed it," Odette said.

"Wonderful Bea," said Grandma Sissy.

Odette set the tray on Grandma Sissy's lap. It had legs that popped out to transform it into a little table. Steam from the tea rose in curlicues and fogged the two little windows of Grandma Sissy's glasses.

Odette didn't know what to do with herself until Grandma Sissy patted the bed. "Sit, sit," she said, and Odette did, feeling a little like a better-trained version of Georgie. She watched Grandma Sissy set aside the tea strainer and pour a stream of cream into the cup. She watched her lift the cup with shaking hands and take a tiny sip.

"Ah," said Grandma Sissy. "Perfect."

Then Grandma Sissy wanted to hear all about the trip — what they'd seen, where they'd been, and how she liked Orcas Island so far.

Odette answered all her questions, and slowly, as

Grandma Sissy drank her tea, Odette's worry drained out of her. She told Grandma Sissy about Rex's latest fury and about her hope that the bookstore down the street might, miraculously, carry animal Cubes.

"Wouldn't that be grand," Grandma Sissy agreed.

But the whole time they talked, Grandma Sissy ate no more than a nibble of the morning bun and held her tea more than she drank it, as if the warmth seeping into her hands from the cup was nourishment enough.

"I am so glad that you're here," said Grandma Sissy, smiling. "The whole family, together. Not to mention, you brought me a breakfast tray, which was very thoughtful of you, even if Bea did arrange it. Now," she said, "why don't you go see if Bea could use any help with the morning rush? The bakery gets pretty busy, you know, as soon as the islanders smell the baking bread. We can talk more later, all right?"

It wasn't all right, not really, but Grandma Sissy looked so tired. "Grandma Sissy?" Odette asked before she left. "Do you remember when you called me, right before we left on our trip?"

"I do," Grandma Sissy said.

"You told me that I might feel powerless over what was

happening to me," Odette said. "But then I had to hang up. I didn't get to hear the rest of what you had to say."

"Yes," Grandma Sissy said. "I remember."

"What was it?"

"I was going to say, you may feel powerless over what is happening to you right now . . . and you are right. You are powerless, sometimes. Sometimes things happen, and we can't stop them from happening."

It was like someone had knocked the air from her chest. Like Grandma Sissy had spoken aloud a grownup truth that grownups never said. That they all knew but wouldn't share.

"Sometimes we are powerless over what life gives us," Grandma Sissy said. "But we have power over what we do with what we're given." She looked right into Odette's eyes. She didn't blink, and Odette felt that Grandma Sissy was trying to tell her something, something extra, besides the words. Odette stared back and tried very, very hard to understand what it was.

Then Grandma Sissy closed her eyes and rested her head against the stack of pillows behind her. "Try not to worry," Grandma Sissy said. "I want you to have fun while you're here, okay?"

Odette nodded again, even though Grandma Sissy's eyes were closed. Given the circumstances, that seemed like a pretty ridiculous request. Like she should have fun knowing that Grandma Sissy had cancer! Like she could do *anything* but worry.

Mastication

THE BAKERY DID get busy, and fast. Bea told Odette that it was a mix of locals and tourists. "More and more tourists," Bea said, "ever since the bakery got that nice review on the Internets."

Odette tried not to laugh about how she said "Internets." It was clear Bea didn't know much about the Web, or computers, or cell phones. She got super irritated when people came into the bakery talking on their phones, especially when they were wearing an earpiece.

"How are you supposed to tell who's talking to you, who's on the phone, and who's just plain crazy?" Bea asked, but it wasn't the kind of question that needed answering.

Bea set Odette to work measuring out ice cream scoops full of cookie dough for baking, and when Mom and Dad came downstairs, she showed them how to work the cash register and refill the display cases. Rex stayed upstairs, either sleeping or playing games on his Game-X.

The bakery grew warmer and warmer as it filled up. A line grew in front of the counter, people jostling for coffee, bread, pastries, and tea.

Lots of people couldn't even wait for a table to dig into their food, biting in right at the register. Crumbs rained down all over the place, and after she was done with the cookie dough, Odette found a broom and set to work.

Mom and Dad kept giving her these proud smiles, all happy that she was pitching in. But Odette didn't feel proud of herself. She felt angry at everyone. All these people, mindlessly shoving pastries in their mouths, messing up Grandma Sissy's floor, when Grandma Sissy herself couldn't even seem to take a bite of her own food.

Chewing, chewing, swallowing, digesting. Masticating. All of it disgusting, and none of it fair.

She swept harder and harder, tear-blurred eyes focused on the black and white tile floor, maneuvering around the customers with a cursory "Excuse me" every so often.

"Odette?"

Odette looked up. Harris. She smiled. "Hey."

"What're you doing?" A really dumb question, considering the broom in her hand.

"Just helping out," Odette said. "This is my grandmother's bakery."

"No way," said Harris. "This place is amazing!" And he took a big bite of his croissant. Somehow, watching *him* eat didn't bother Odette at all. "It's really cool," he said, "running into you like this."

"Yeah," Odette answered. "Pretty strange."

"I was going to text you after breakfast," Harris said. "I didn't want to wake you up."

"I've been up for hours," said Odette, and they stood there in the middle of the bakery, Harris holding his half-eaten croissant, Odette holding the broom. They were awkward and quiet for a minute, but even though it was uncomfortable, Odette didn't want Harris to leave. "Hey," she blurted, kind of loud. "Do you want to meet my dog?"

"Sure," he answered. And smiled.

Walking Tour

HARRIS SAID GEORGIE was adorable. "Can we take her for a walk?" he asked.

"Okay," said Odette, even though it hadn't been all that long since their morning outing.

"Mom," Odette said, "remember Harris from the ferry?"

"Sure," Mom said. "Hi there."

"We're going to take Georgie on a walk, okay?"

"Sounds good. Have fun," she said.

The rain had stopped and the sky was blue-gray and wide open. Georgie, despite her earlier walk, wagged her tail and strained against her harness.

The farther into the island they walked, the prettier the buildings seemed to get. Here in Eastsound the houses lined up like ladies at an old-fashioned dance, side by side in blue and yellow and violet, their windows trimmed in brightly contrasting colors like ribbons, bright red roofs topping them.

Peekaboo views of the ocean popped up here and there, but even when Odette couldn't see the water, there was a knowledge of it, all around, encircling them. Cozy and cut off from the rest of the world, the island felt magical. Maybe that explained the feeling Odette had inside, the jostling, unnerving hopefulness about nothing in particular, the excitement simmering in her heart.

Or maybe it was because of the boy walking next to her, his hands shoved into his jacket pockets, and the way his eyes roamed around, taking everything in; the way when his gaze landed on her looking at him, he smiled, kind of goofy and shy.

They walked and walked. As they walked they compared favorites — favorite movie, favorite book, favorite song, favorite sport. None of their favorites aligned. Harris liked action movies, and mystery books, and rap, and basketball. But it was okay. They both seemed to like walking just fine.

Finally they came to a bench that overlooked the ocean, and without discussing it they both flopped down.

Georgie seemed tired too, and she hopped right up on Odette's lap, curling into a little ball.

"This is fun," Harris said. "I like it here."

Odette wondered if he meant "here" on Orcas Island or "here" next to her. "Me too," she said.

And then Harris did this thing Odette had seen in movies—he stretched his right arm along the back of the bench, behind Odette's shoulders. Was this his way of putting an arm around her, or was he just stretching? There was no way to tell—until Odette looked at his face, and then it seemed pretty clear from his expression, his soft eyes. Was this it? Would this be her first kiss, here, on this bench, in this very moment?

"I'd better get back," Odette said, a little louder than she'd meant to, and she stood up fast. Georgie tumbled to the ground, landing awkwardly and grunting her disapproval. "See you later." Odette yanked on Georgie's leash and had to force herself to just walk, not run.

Terminal

GRANDMA SISSY DIDN'T get out of bed until the bakery closed just after two o'clock. Bea stayed the whole time, and two other people helped out as well, a lady named Charlotte, older than Grandma Sissy but younger than Bea, who brought supplies from the ferry, and a guy about Mom and Dad's age named Gary, who came to prep for the next morning. He was a snappy dresser: dark jeans cuffed at the ankle, a purple-gray button-down shirt with the sleeves rolled above his elbows. Black suspenders, brown leather boots.

Odette imagined Harris in a pair of suspenders, and then shook her head. What was wrong with her? There was Grandma Sissy, sitting at the table, barely able to eat half a sandwich, and Odette was obsessing over a boy she hardly knew.

Not one of the people who came to help seemed to be

working *for* Grandma Sissy; the best Odette could figure out, they were all just friends of hers who wanted to help. She'd always thought that an island would be a really lonely place to live, but Grandma Sissy seemed to be surrounded by people who cared about her.

"So, what sights will you see while you're here?" Grandma Sissy asked. "You can rent bicycles . . . there's whale watching . . . oh, and my good friend Helen-Marie has a farm on the south side of the island. She says you can come visit anytime and even stay the night if you'd like!" She smiled brightly.

"Mom," said Odette's mom, "we need to talk. Not about activities. About you."

"Maybe the kids should go outside," Dad said, "while we talk."

"Can Gary walk me over to the art gallery?" Rex asked. "He told me it's full of dolphin sculptures right now."

"I'm sure he'd be happy to," Grandma Sissy said. "Odette, do you want to go with them?"

"No," she said. "I'm staying here."

"Go with your brother, Detters," Mom said.

"I want to say here," Odette said, feeling stubborn but not wanting to back down.

"Let her stay, Liz," Grandma Sissy said. "She's old enough to know her own mind."

Mom opened her mouth to protest again, but Dad said, "Okay, sure, you can stay, Odette," and when Mom shot him a look he said, "She's getting pretty grown up, honey. Let her stay."

So it was just Rex who headed off with Gary, which was weird because back at home there was *no way* Mom would have let him leave the house with someone who was practically a stranger. Back home, Mom barely let *anyone* look after Rex. Last year on their wedding anniversary, Mom and Dad had been all dressed up to go out to dinner when the one sitter Rex liked called and canceled because she was throwing up. And even though Dad wanted her to, Mom refused to call another sitter. "Caroline's the only one who can calm him down other than us," she said. And Dad looked mad and disappointed and Mom took off her high heels and no one went anywhere that night.

After Rex left with Gary, Mom turned to Grandma Sissy and asked, "How long?"

"I didn't want to tell you over the phone," Grandma

Sissy said, "and I knew you were on your way. There was no point in going into details until you got here."

"No *point?*" Mom's voice went way up, sharp and shrill. "You should have told me sooner how bad it is. How far it's gone." She shook her head.

"Lizzy, there is not one thing you could have done," said Grandma Sissy. "Not everything can be fixed."

"But—I'm your daughter!" Mom wailed.

"That is true with or without the cancer," Grandma Sissy said. "That will be true even after I am gone."

"It's too soon to talk about *that,*" Mom said, but next to her, Dad didn't look so sure. He patted her back like he didn't know what else to do.

"It's not too soon," Grandma Sissy said. "Definitely not." She paused for a moment, and then said, "Liz, the doctor is calling it stage four."

That didn't mean anything to Odette, but she could tell by the expression on her parents' faces that it wasn't good.

"How long?" Mom asked again.

"How long until what?" Odette said. "Are you going to be okay? Are you going to get better?"

Grandma Sissy looked straight at Odette, her eyes

appraising. "What have your parents told you?" she asked.

"Just that you're sick," Odette said. "But you were sick before. And you got better then, right?"

Grandma Sissy sighed. "Yes," she said. "Last time, I got better. This time, I won't."

"You won't get better?" Odette said. "But . . . you don't need an appendix, right? Why don't they just take it out?"

Grandma Sissy pinched her nose between her fingers. Then she looked at Odette. "Darling," she said, "when the doctors went in to take my appendix, they found cancer everywhere. There was nothing for them to do but close me back up."

"So . . . what now?" Odette asked. "Is there medicine they can give you?"

Grandma Sissy shook her head. "I did all the treatments last time," she said, "with the breast cancer. I'm not afraid of pain, Odette. I don't like pain, but it doesn't scare me. If treatments would make me better, I would do them. But, Odette," she said again, "not everything can be fixed. Sometimes, the toothpaste is out of the tube." She smiled at Odette, one of those sad sideways smiles that grownups sometimes did when there was nothing to smile about. "Darling, I am going to die. That is the fact of the matter. The question is not if. It is when."

Beside her, Odette's mom shook almost silently, as if she was trying to hold herself together but couldn't quite manage it. "How long?" she asked.

"Not long," Grandma Sissy said. She spoke gently.

"We're not ready," Mom sobbed. "We haven't had enough time."

"We have today," Grandma Sissy said.

End Call

I MISS YOU SO much," Odette said into the phone.

She'd called Mieko to tell her about Grandma Sissy, but when Mieko answered the phone with her chirpy voice and questions about Harris, Odette suddenly didn't want to talk about anything—not about Grandma Sissy, not about their trip, and certainly not about what had almost happened with Harris on the bench.

She just wanted to *listen,* but Mieko insisted that she had nothing interesting to say. "My sisters are driving me crazy," she said. "It's hot here. It's boring."

Then there was silence that felt like a challenge.

Odette met it with her own wall of stony nothingness. She could be quiet too. But after a minute she caved in. "I miss you so much," she said.

"I miss you, too," said Mieko, grudgingly. "But jeez, Odette, you're on the trip of a lifetime."

"You don't know anything!" Odette burst out.

"Fine," said Mieko, her voice just as angry. "If I don't know anything, then why do you even call me all the time?"

And it struck Odette that she *had* been the one doing most of the calling. Anger and shame filled her all the way up to her ears. "Maybe I *won't,* then," she said, and slammed her thumb against the End button.

In Real Life

OUT FRONT, GARY was teaching Rex how to play jacks. They'd bought a set at the bookstore down the street.

"Do they sell Cubes there?" Odette asked.

"No," said Rex. "Why would they?"

"I just thought it would be cool if they did," Odette said. "You know, if they had a Whales, Porpoises, and Dolphins one just waiting for you to buy it."

"That kind of stuff never happens in real life," Rex said.

"But it would be cool if it did," Odette said.

"I guess." Rex tracked the bouncy ball with his eyes, scooping up sets of jacks after each bounce. "Watch this," he said. "I can do foursies."

Primates Cube

THE NEXT MORNING, Harris came back into Sissy's Bakery. He smiled at Odette from one side of the counter and asked if she would please sell him a chocolate croissant, slightly warm if they had any that were still warm.

"Thanks," Harris said, taking the croissant.

"No problem," Odette said.

Then they just stood there. Harris scratched his head and looked at his croissant, not stepping away from the counter, even though there was a line of people behind him. Finally, he said, "Hey. I'm leaving tomorrow morning, early. Do you want to go for a walk or something?"

"I'm busy right now," said Odette, which was true; Bea had been in the kitchen since before dawn, and this time when Odette had finished taking Georgie for a walk, instead of offering her a morning bun, Bea had set Odette straight to work. "There's lots for you to learn, and I aim to teach you," she had said.

"Okay," Harris said. "Maybe later?"

"Okay." Odette smiled, and Harris smiled, and with all the smiling and plan-making she forgot to charge him for the croissant and he forgot to pay.

That morning, Rex had taken the breakfast tray in to Grandma Sissy. He'd told Odette that she'd been almost asleep the whole time and hadn't eaten a bite.

"That's how you know when an animal is getting ready to die," Rex said, all matter-of-fact, in front of Mom and everyone. "They stop eating."

"Grandma Sissy isn't an animal," Odette had said.

"Sure she is," Rex said. "We all are. We're mammals. Primates. Most closely related to chimps, bonobos, gorillas, and orangutans. There were even little plastic *Homo sapiens* in my Primates Cube, mixed together with the great apes."

Maybe technically that was true—that people were animals, mammals, primates. But weren't they more than that too?

A picture occurred to Odette suddenly, of a giant gorilla being bitten in the neck by a zombie. What would happen then? Could a gorilla be zombified? Could Grandma Sissy? Would a zombie Grandma Sissy be better than no Grandma Sissy at all?

Photo Op

WHEN THE MORNING crowd dispersed, Mom and Dad decided a family outing was in order. It would do them all good, is how Dad put it.

They walked through downtown Eastsound, following the same path Odette had walked the day before with Harris.

When Rex asked where they were going, Mom just answered, "You'll see."

They didn't walk very far before they arrived at a small white-shingled building. Dad opened the door, ushering them inside. STILLWATER KAYAK TOURS read the sign.

"Awesome," said Rex.

The woman who worked there was expecting them. She already had a life vest in each of their sizes picked out, and when they came into the shop, she zipped up her waterproof jacket and said, "Right on time!"

Dad signed a few forms and then they each pulled on a life vest, even the woman, who said her name was Laura Beth and that she'd be their guide.

"You're going to go kayaking with us?" Rex asked.

"Uh-huh. You guys will row double kayaks, and I'll come along in a single to show you the sights. Okay?"

"Sure," said Rex. "Do you know all about the animals that live around here?"

"I do," Laura Beth answered. "If we're lucky, we'll see a bunch of them today."

Down by the shore, Laura Beth gave each of them a paddle and showed them how to dip in one blade and then the other to propel the kayaks forward. "Lighter person in the front, heavier person in the back," she said, and just like that, Odette found herself in a kayak with Mom, Laura Beth wading ankle-deep to cast them off before scrambling into a kayak of her own.

It wasn't hard to maneuver the kayak; Laura Beth showed them how to go forward, backwards, left, and right—and the water glistened smooth and shiny all around.

They hugged the shoreline, venturing just far enough out so that their paddles wouldn't strike the sand, and then headed east. Water birds dipped and swayed. Droplets splashed up from the blades onto the bow of the boat, casting impossibly tiny rainbows.

It felt so good to dip the blade of her paddle into the water, to pull through each stroke. In the kayak, perched just above the surface of the ocean, Odette felt wonderfully alive.

"There's a heron." Laura Beth gestured with the dripping tip of her paddle to the shoreline. The bird stood in tall reeds about ten feet in from the waterline, its yellow eyes tracking them.

"Is that a great blue?" Rex asked, excited.

"It sure is," said Laura Beth. She sounded surprised. "How did you know?"

"I like birds," Rex answered.

Dad, behind him in the kayak, told Laura Beth, "Rex has always had a knack for animal identification."

Odette turned to keep watching the bird as they paddled past it. It was a big bird, with long legs and knobby knees, a sheet of gray-blue feathers, and a pointed orange bill. It didn't look friendly, but it did look smart.

On and on they rowed, and though the sky was overcast it didn't rain, and Odette was warm enough. Here and there Laura Beth called out an animal, but more often Rex beat her to it, announcing each seagull and heron with mounting excitement. When a wide-winged bald eagle cut across the sky, Rex was so thrilled that his hands forgot to keep holding his paddle.

"I can't believe it," he said over and over. "I just can't believe it."

If you asked Odette, Laura Beth looked pretty annoyed with Rex as she fished Rex's paddle out of the water with her own.

After a while, Dad maneuvered his and Rex's kayak up close to Mom and Odette's. They rowed along side by side, their paddles tapping together every now and then. Laura Beth led the way, her kayak pulling farther and farther ahead.

"So," Dad began when Laura Beth was out of earshot. And that was when Odette figured out that they'd planned this—getting her and Rex out on the water and into a good mood, so that they could have some big "talk."

"You both know Grandma Sissy is sick," said Dad.

"She's dying," said Rex, matter-of-fact, and then, "Oh, look! A fish!"

That's just how Rex was. It was how he'd always been.

"Yes," Dad said, and Mom started to cry behind Odette. Her crying made the boat vibrate a little. "She's dying."

"She might live for a long time," Odette argued. "Sometimes even people who are really sick get better."

Mom reached over and rubbed Odette's shoulder. Odette felt like shrugging away her hand, but she didn't. "Detters," Mom said, "Grandma Sissy isn't going to get better."

"You can't know that!" Odette said. A hot flush climbed up her neck and spread across her face. Her mom's hand felt like a giant spider on her shoulder. "She might get better."

"Kids," Dad said, "your grandmother has made a decision. One that you might not understand, but I want you to hear what we need to tell you, okay?"

Odette nodded. She had a terrible feeling, even though she had no idea what Dad could be talking about.

"Sometimes," Dad said, "bad things happen. And not everything can be fixed."

"That's what Grandma Sissy says," Odette answered. It was weird to hear Grandma Sissy's words coming out of Dad's mouth.

"Right," Dad said. Then he seemed to run out of words. Mom picked up where he left off. "Sometimes," she said, squeezing Odette's shoulder, "when you love someone, you have to let them go."

"Grandma Sissy can't go anywhere," Rex said. "She can barely get out of bed."

"I don't think they're talking about Grandma Sissy taking a trip," Odette said, finally shrugging Mom's hand off her shoulder. "Right?"

And then Mom and Dad told them about how Washington was a right-to-die state, how if someone had less than six months to live, they could get medicine that would make it so they could die peacefully, at home, before the pain became unbearable. They said that this was what Grandma Sissy had decided to do, and that she had filled the prescription.

"That's legal?" Odette asked. "She can just . . . *kill* herself?"

"Detters," Mom said, and Odette could hear how hard she was trying to stay calm, the way she did when Rex was having one of his furies. "Cancer is killing Grandma Sissy. She isn't going to get better. She's only going to get sicker, and no matter what, she is going to die."

Cancer, thought Odette, should get the top spot on her list of Things That Aren't Fair.

"She will stay with us as long as she can," Dad said. "She'll stay until the pain gets to be too much."

Laura Beth was paddling back toward them. She gestured with the blade of her paddle. "Check out that big rock," she called. "There's a mama seal and her baby."

Sure enough, two gray blobs — a big one and a smaller one right beside it — lay spread across the top of a rounded rock that jutted from the water.

It seemed ridiculous to look at seals right now. But Rex loved wildlife more than anything in the world, and the appearance of the seals seemed to erase Grandma Sissy from his mind. "Mom," he hissed, trying to be quiet, "take a picture!" He bounced in the kayak. It rocked back and forth, threatening to tip, and Dad did his best to steady them with his oar.

"Calm down, buddy," he said.

Odette felt trapped on the kayaks, trapped with her family, trapped with the terrible thing that her parents had just said.

Mom fumbled in her pocket to pull out the cell phone. All of a sudden it seemed that nothing mattered to any of them other than getting Rex his picture. It was *insane,* Odette thought.

Their kayak drifted too close to the rock, and the mama seal got nervous. She nudged the baby with her bristly snout and it slid into the water. She headed in after it.

"Hurry, Mom!" wailed Rex.

Mom slid her thumb across the cell phone's screen to unlock it, but then a truly terrible thing happened. The phone slipped from her hand and tumbled—*splash!*—beneath the surface of the water.

Odette watched, open-mouthed, as it sank until it disappeared.

"Mom!" yelled Rex, on the edge of a fury. "Now we can't get a picture!"

"That's why wrist straps are such a good idea," said Laura Beth, completely unhelpfully.

Odette was so mad, she wanted to scream right along with Rex. She wanted to throw her paddle. She wanted to tip the kayak and dump Mom into the ocean. She wanted to disappear, to be anywhere but here.

And then she realized that without the phone, she couldn't call Harris. She had no idea where he was staying. If he tried to call her, she wouldn't be able to answer. He'd think she was avoiding him. And he was leaving the island tomorrow.

One Stupid Phone

"I DON'T UNDERSTAND WHY you're so upset, Detters," said Mom as they climbed out of the kayaks. "It's just a phone. A hunk of plastic and wiring."

Even through her angry tears, Odette heard the implication: She shouldn't be distraught over a dumb phone when her own grandmother was dying. But knowing that didn't help her to feel better about the lost phone; it only made her feel worse about herself.

"I'm not upset about the cell phone," Odette lied, wiping tears from her cheeks. "But if we didn't have one stupid family phone, it wouldn't matter at all."

"This is disappointing, Detters." Mom *looked* disappointed. Her hair, damp from the persistent misty rain that had begun while they were still out kayaking, hung across her forehead in drippy strands. Her shoulders curved limply, and her whole body seemed to radiate disappointment.

"Take it easy, Liz," Dad said. "It's okay that she's upset about the phone."

"I'm not upset about the phone!" Odette yelled— actually *yelled*. She hardly ever yelled. No one had ever told her, but Odette knew—she had always known—that it was her job to stay calm. To be the good one.

But she yelled now, and her hands in tight fists shook with anger—her whole body shook—and then she ran, sprinting away from the trio of her family, leaving them behind on the sidewalk of Eastsound Village on Orcas Island in Washington State, one of the only places in the entire world where someone's grandmother could talk a doctor into giving her medicine to commit suicide, which didn't make any sense, none at all.

She ran and ran, sprinting straight past Grandma Sissy's bakery. She ran as the rain came down harder. She ran, and even though people on the sidewalks looked at her like she had totally lost her mind, she didn't stop running, didn't swerve from her path, willing everyone to get out of her way.

Odette ran until her fists loosened and her legs felt rubbery and weak. At last, she stopped. Pretty houses lined the street, their doors a palette of colors, red and blue and black and green. Odette put her hands on her knees and gasped until her heart calmed down, until her throat unclenched. How the heck was it even possible that she had come so far from home? So far from school, and Mieko, and routine and safety and her own little life. Her cheeks were damp with mist and sweat and tears.

Eventually, she wiped her cheeks and walked slowly back to Grandma Sissy's house. She stood outside the bakery door, not wanting to go in yet.

Somewhere on the island a clock rang out, sending four loud "dongs" into the misty air. It was four o'clock in the afternoon. By this time tomorrow, Harris would be long gone.

Time seemed to be going too fast, and Odette felt paralyzed by her inability to slow it down.

She saw again, like a little movie, the phone slipping out of Mom's hand and splashing into the water. She remembered Harris's arm looping across the bench behind her shoulders and the little shiver of pleasure shooting up her spine. But then she thought of Grandma Sissy's stomach, the way it jutted out. She imagined her list, and how if she was being honest, the lost phone would appear on it too, right underneath "Cancer."

She shook her head hard to make all of it go away, but she was left with a terrible question: How could she be considering kissing a boy when her grandmother was so very sick? What kind of a person was she?

Upstairs

NO ONE WAS in the bakery. Upstairs, Odette found her family sitting at the spindle-legged wooden table in front of the fireplace, working on a puzzle. Rex had sorted out three piles of blues in different shades, and Dad was working on doing the edges. Mom just kept picking up random pieces and trying to fit them together, a strategy that should have been ineffectual. She was strangely lucky, though, finding more matches that way than Odette would have thought statistically possible.

Grandma Sissy sat in the soft armchair nearby, her feet on a leather footstool, a fuzzy soft blanket across her legs. Georgie seemed right at home on her lap, curled into her usual little ball.

They looked like a picture, the whole bunch of them. Right then, no one could have guessed at all the bad stuff—Dad being laid off, and Mom getting so irritated with Odette, and Rex's furies, and Grandma Sissy dying. Odette stood in the doorway and watched them like she was looking at a painting hanging in a museum, standing extra still so no one would notice her.

Then she remembered afresh about the sunken phone and how Harris would probably be trying to get ahold of her, wondering why she wasn't answering or returning his call, and the warmth she was feeling seeped away. Grandma Sissy looked up, as if she could sense the change in the atmosphere, and saw her.

"There you are, darling," she said. "You are sopping wet."

Odette shrugged. "I guess I'll go take a bath."

"That sounds nice," Grandma Sissy said. "Use the purple bath salts in the medicine cabinet. They smell like violets."

The Belly of the Beast

GRANDMA SISSY HAD one of those old-fashioned bathtubs that was raised up from the floor by four clawed feet, each clutching a ball. The hot and cold water came out of two separate spouts rather than mixing together in the faucet and coming out warm.

Odette plugged the drain with the rubber stopper that hung from a chain on the edge of the bathtub and then cranked on both faucets, getting the temperature just right. Then she pulled off her wet clothes and found a fluffy towel in the cabinet next to the toilet. She had just dunked her toes in the filling tub when she remembered the bath salts. The medicine cabinet was old-fashioned too, painted mint green, with a beveled mirror on the front made of wavy glass, and a tiny twist lock to open it.

Inside, the three shelves were carefully arranged, with

powders and perfumes on the bottom shelf, bath salts and oils on the second, and on the top, clear orange plastic pill bottles, each wrapped in a sticker from the pharmacy detailing the name of the medication and instructions for use. Odette wondered if one of the bottles held the pills that Grandma Sissy could take when she decided it was time to die.

Was that selfish — to die on purpose and leave people behind, people who loved you? Was it selfish of Odette to want Grandma Sissy to stay, despite her pain? A rush of heat flooded Odette as she considered taking all the bottles and opening them, shaking the pills into the toilet and flushing them away. She could do it. It would only take a moment.

Instead, Odette took the bath salts and closed the cabinet. She watched her hand as if it were someone else's, unstopping the jar and shaking the purple crystals into the water.

The water steamed around her legs as Odette stepped into the tub. Slowly, she lowered herself in. Remembering the tub's four clawed feet, Odette imagined she had climbed inside the belly of a great beast. She closed her eyes and rested her head against the bathtub's curved edge.

Suddenly she thought of Mieko's cat. He had been hit by a car two summers ago. The car hadn't killed him, but it had crushed his back legs and broken his back, and the vet had said the cat would never be able to walk again. And Odette remembered how sad that was, but also how glad she'd been that the vet could help him die.

If Grandma Sissy were a cat, or even an ape, or a dog, or a ferret—then the answer would be easy. An animal in pain had to be put to sleep.

But Grandma Sissy wasn't an ape, or a dog, or a ferret, or a cat. She was a grandmother. She was a mother, and a baker, and a friend.

Confessions

THE BATH DIDN'T make her feel better. Emerging from
the water twenty minutes later, Odette still felt anger
at her mother for losing the phone, worry over Grandma
Sissy's sickness and the pills in the cabinet, guilt over not
being able to answer Harris's call, and lonely sadness
about her fight with Mieko.

She got dressed in her pajamas and then went back out
to the room where Rex and her parents were still working on the puzzle. They'd made progress; the edge was
completely finished, framing a square of the tabletop,
and large sections of the middle had been connected too.
Odette could see what looked to be a snowy mountain in
the top right corner.

Grandma Sissy was asleep, still in her chair, with
Georgie on her lap. One of her hands rested on Georgie's
back. Her fingers were long and thin. The skin on the

backs of her hands was a rainbow of bruises and bumps, purple and green and black.

"What's the matter with her hands?" Odette asked.

"Her skin is just really fragile," Mom answered. "She bruises easily now."

Odette wondered if this was because of the cancer or because of all the medicines, but she didn't want to ask. How could she have gotten this weak so quickly? On her last visit to their house, she'd had tons of energy for walks around the neighborhood and a trip to the beach and a day at Disneyland. Odette had sat on a stool in their kitchen and watched as Grandma Sissy had baked their favorite cookies—snickerdoodles for Rex and double chocolate chip for Odette.

"Do you want to do the puzzle with us?" Dad asked.

Odette said no and lowered herself to the rug in front of the fire, by Grandma Sissy's chair. She watched the flames eat at the log. She watched it blacken as it threw off heat. Soon the log would be gone, and the warmth of the fire would fade, and only ashes would remain.

She felt a hand on her hair and looked up. Grandma Sissy was awake. "You look just like your mother did at your age," Grandma Sissy said.

Tears welled up in Odette's eyes.

"Oh, darling," Grandma Sissy said. "It's all right. You don't need to be so sad."

And that was even worse—that Grandma Sissy thought Odette was only upset because of the cancer. She couldn't stand to lie like that, to her grandmother, so Odette admitted, "Right now, Grandma Sissy, I'm crying because Mom lost our cell phone in the ocean." A wave of shame hit her square in the chest, and her tears turned to sobs. "I'm such a terrible person," she said. How could she care about such stupid things—a phone and a boy and a fight with her friend—when Grandma Sissy was dying?

And then the words poured out—how she was supposed to see Harris, and probably he'd called, and now he'd think she was avoiding him, and he was leaving in the morning for Fidalgo Island and he'd never know she had *wanted* to go on another walk, and that maybe even she wanted to kiss him, and that she was a rotten, terrible, selfish person for caring about any of this right now at all when she was also so sad and scared about Grandma Sissy, and she was sorry, she was so, so sorry.

When she looked up at last, all her confessions made,

she expected to see a look of disappointment on Grandma Sissy's face. But her grandmother was smiling.

"My darling," she said, "it is perfectly all right to be sad and scared about my dying and at the same time to want to kiss that boy. That's life, you know; the good stuff and the bad stuff all mixed up together."

"You wanted to *kiss* that guy?" Rex said. "But you just met him!"

And that made everybody laugh, which was okay with Odette because it didn't feel like they were laughing *at* her, and then her parents left the puzzle and came to sit with her in front of the fire. Rex came too, plopping down practically on top of Odette.

"I'm sorry I dropped the phone, Detters," Mom said.

"It's okay," Odette said. "It was just an accident."

"You know," said Grandma Sissy, "Orcas Island isn't very big. There aren't very many places where Harris could be staying. I know just about everyone on Orcas, including all the people who run the hotels. I'll bet I could track him down."

"Or we could put a sign in the bakery window, in case he comes by in the morning," said Mom. "It could say, 'Odette to Harris: Phone Lost! Please Come Inside!'"

"We could all go outside and walk around yelling his name," Rex suggested. "Probably he'd come out eventually."

Odette laughed. They all sounded like perfectly awful ideas. "He'll think I'm crazy," she said. "I'd feel like an idiot."

Grandma Sissy said, "In my experience, it's better to feel foolish now than to feel sorry later."

That was just like Grandma Sissy, to have a little saying that went with the situation. In a flash, Odette knew that she'd always remember the funny little sayings — always, even after Grandma Sissy had died, even when Odette had become a grownup herself. Because those things were going to happen, as Grandma Sissy said, whether Odette wanted them to or not. "I feel better just talking about it," Odette said. "Thank you, guys."

Grandma Sissy petted her hair again, and Dad hugged her, and Mom smiled. Rex just shrugged and went back to the puzzle, but that was okay too. And right then, though Odette knew the feeling wouldn't last, even with the lost phone and Mieko being mad at her and Grandma Sissy's being sick, even with all of that, everything felt just fine.

An Affirmation

"ODETTE."

She tried to open her eyes, but they were still crusty with sleep.

"Odette. Wake up." It was her dad.

Slowly, Odette peeled open her eyes. The room was barely light. By her feet, Georgie groaned and rolled over.

"Dad?"

"Everything's fine, Odette. But come on, get up."

Odette slid her legs out from under Georgie and tip-toed around Rex. She followed Dad into the front room. "What is it?" she asked.

"I found a ferry schedule," Dad said, smiling. "And look . . ." He held a trifold paper under the table lamp next to Grandma Sissy's chair. "A boat is leaving for Anacortes—that's on Fidalgo Island—at six forty-five this morning. Isn't that where you said Harris was heading next?"

"Umm . . ." said Odette. Was her dad really suggesting that she race to the dock to track down a boy she had only met a few times? *Her* dad, the cautious one, who always double-checked everything and warned them "Be careful" at every turn?

"Odette, let me tell you something," Dad said. "Taking that voluntary layoff was the scariest thing I've ever done. It was a leap into the void. But you know what else it was? An affirmation of life. I haven't been one to take many chances, honey, but the only chances I regret are the ones I *didn't* take." He held up her jacket, which Odette hadn't noticed was in his hand. "Come on," he said. "It'll be fun."

Probably it wouldn't be fun. It didn't *sound* fun. It sounded embarrassing and terrifying. But just the same, she liked that Dad had come to wake her up. She liked that everyone in her family wanted to help. And Odette saw that this was about more than whether or not she got to Harris before the boat left. This was about adventure. Taking a chance.

"What the heck," she said, and shoved her arms into her jacket.

Angry Lobster Pajamas

GRANDMA SISSY'S CAR was a funny old station wagon, square-backed and sputtering. When they pulled it out of the garage, Odette saw that the windshield was dusty. She wondered when her grandmother had last driven. This was the first time Odette had been in a regular car since they'd left home and begun their trip in the Coach, and it felt kind of strange. Cramped, almost. With a shot of surprise, Odette realized that she actually *missed* their traveling home.

They headed down Main Street, waving at Gary as he walked toward the bakery to help Bea with the morning rush, and turned left onto Orcas Road. Then it was pretty much a straight drive down the island to the ferry station, not very far at all. The sun filled the sky.

Maybe because it was an early ferry, the dock wasn't

very crowded. Dad pulled the car up as close as he could to the ticket booth. "Do you see him?" he asked.

Odette shook her head. She didn't see Harris any-where—until she did. "There." She pointed. It was Harris, absolutely, walking with his back to her, but with his left shoulder just a bit higher than his right, his fuzzy hair all tall in the middle.

"Well, what are you waiting for?" Dad asked, grinning.

Odette opened the car door and stumble-fell right onto the pavement. She scraped both of her palms but stood up and ran toward Harris without even looking at her hands, swiping them across the legs of her—oh, no—her pajamas. She was still wearing her angry lobster pajamas. And no wonder she tripped: she was wearing her candy striped slipper socks, the ones with the moccasin bot-toms.

In a flash, Odette considered turning back to the car. There was still time—Harris hadn't seen her, so she could get away without him knowing she'd tracked him down, without him seeing her ridiculous pajamas.

But then she remembered what her dad had said, about chances, and she remembered Grandma Sissy's words, too—*Better to feel foolish now than to feel sorry later*—and before she could talk herself out of it, Odette cupped her mouth with her hands and yelled, "Harris!"

He stopped. He turned and lifted his hand to shade his eyes, scanning the dock. Then he saw her. He smiled.

Odette half jogged, half walked, to close the distance between them. "Hey," she said.

"Hey," he said back.

"I wasn't ditching you or avoiding your calls," Odette blurted. "But we went kayaking and then Rex saw these seals and he wanted Mom to take a picture and now our one family cell phone is at the bottom of the ocean."

Harris's eyebrows went up. "Wow," he said.

"I mean—" Odette had a terrible thought. "That is, if you even called me. If you did, I didn't get your calls, obviously. If you didn't . . ." She wasn't sure how to finish this sentence.

"No, I did," said Harris. "I did call. A few times, actually." His smile was kind of shy. "I'm glad to hear you didn't get them. I was starting to worry you were avoiding me."

"Yeah. That's why I'm here. My dad drove me." Odette pointed out her dad, still sitting in the car.

Harris waved at him. Dad waved back.

"Anyway," said Odette, "I'm sorry we couldn't go on that walk. That's all. I just wanted to tell you that."

"That's really cool that you drove all the way down here, early and everything, to find me," Harris said. "It's, like, from a movie or something."

"Yeah," said Odette, but unlike people in the movies, she had no idea what to do next. She saw Harris's mom a little ways ahead, waiting for him. "Anyway," she said again, "maybe we could still call each other and stuff, I mean, when I get another phone."

"Cool," said Harris. He dug a receipt out of his pocket and found a pen in his backpack and scribbled down his number. Odette folded the receipt twice and tucked it into her jacket pocket. Then it was time to say goodbye, and Harris looked as nervous as she felt. Odette kind of wanted to kiss him, but both his mom and her dad were watching and she wasn't really sure how to kiss, anyway, at least not the boyfriend kind of kissing.

So instead she lurched forward awkwardly and gave him a quick hug, a squeeze with a double back pat, and then let go.

Harris smiled bigger and said, "It was really nice

meeting you, Odette." Then he waved and turned away, catching up with his mom.

Odette knew she was blushing, but she didn't care. And she felt totally silly in her ridiculous lobster pajamas. But Dad and Grandma Sissy were right. She was really glad she'd come.

Back at the bakery she told her story over and over again, first to Bea, who was behind the counter in the kitchen—"Good for you, hon," Bea said—and then upstairs to Mom and Rex, who were just finishing up the puzzle (it was an old European castle), and finally to Grandma Sissy when she took in the tray.

"He looked totally shocked to see me," Odette told her. "But happy, too."

"I'm so proud of you, my darling," said Grandma Sissy. Her breathing seemed like it hurt her today, like each breath cost her something, but her smile was sincere. "Did you know," Grandma Sissy said, and Odette had to lean in close to hear all her words, "that I was there when you were born?"

"Yes," said Odette. "Mom told me." Her dad had been away on business, and there should have been plenty of time for him to get home before the due date, but Odette's mom's water had broken and her contractions started and Dad hadn't been able to make it all the way from New York in time.

"It was my good luck that I was visiting your mom," Grandma Sissy said. "I was there in the room with her and the midwife when you came into the world. I remember it perfectly. Your dark little head. Your red squished-up face. And when you opened your eyes . . ." Sissy shook her head. "It was like looking in the mirror and seeing my very own soul. Me, your mother, you. Maybe one day you'll have a daughter, hmm? And maybe she'll have the same eyes too."

Grandma Sissy looked like she was going to say more, but then she closed her eyes. "I think I'll sleep a little," she said, and then, "I'm proud of you, my darling."

Every Day

I T HIT ODETTE while she was putting away the cookie sheets after she and Gary had finished baking for the day: Mieko didn't know about the phone.

It was true that they'd fought, but it was also true that they were best friends.

She had to call Mieko. She had to call at once.

"Gary, I need to go," she said, closing the pantry and wiping her hands on her apron.

"Okay, then," he said. Nothing ever seemed to bother Gary, and he always looked so fancy. Today he was wearing purple corduroy trousers and a light pink shirt under a dark pink sweater vest.

"Gary." Odette paused before heading upstairs. "How come you always dress so nice?"

"Because every day is a special occasion," he answered.

"How can every day be special?" Odette asked.

"Doesn't that kind of go against the whole idea of what 'special' means?"

Gary untied his apron and folded it neatly. "Every day is special," he said, "because you only get one chance at it."

"That sounds like a lot of pressure."

"I suppose that's one way to look at it," said Gary.

Upstairs, Odette used Grandma Sissy's home phone to call Mieko. Hers was one number Odette had memorized; she had been dialing it for the last three years, since the Christmas they were both ten and they had each gotten a cell phone. Even though Odette had it programmed in her phone, she liked to punch in the pattern of numbers that connected her to her friend.

It rang three times before Mieko answered, and when she did, it was with a tentative "Hello?"

"Mieko, it's me."

"Odette!" Mieko shrieked so loudly that Odette had to hold the phone away from her ear, but she didn't complain. "Oh my god, I thought something terrible had happened to you! I called and called and you never called me back. I must have left you, like, a hundred messages. I thought your island had sunk or something."

"Not the island," Odette said. "Just the phone." And she

plopped on Grandma Sissy's chair and told Mieko every-thing: about the phone sinking in the ocean and Harris and her ridiculous lobster pajama bottoms and Grandma Sissy being so sick. She explained to Mieko about the Death with Dignity Act, about the bottles of medication in Grandma Sissy's bathroom cabinet.

"But that's just *awful*," Mieko said.

Part of Odette agreed, but another part didn't. "I don't know," she said. "What about your cat?"

"That was different," Mieko said. "He was an *animal*."

Then they were quiet again, but they were still together on the phone. Odette liked that, knowing that Mieko was right there.

"Hey, Odette?"

"Yeah?"

"I'm sorry about the other day. About what I said."

"Me too," said Odette.

In the Kitchen

A FEW DAYS LATER, Grandma Sissy came downstairs to the bakery. Dad walked in front of her, and Grandma Sissy used his shoulder as support, clutching the railing with her other hand, and Mom walked right behind her, keeping her hands on Grandma Sissy's waist just in case she lost her balance.

Odette watched from the bottom of the staircase, holding open the door that led to the bakery. She thought about all the times she'd run up and down stairs in her life, never giving it a thought.

When at last Grandma Sissy reached the bottom, Mom lowered her into a chair that they'd moved into the kitchen area. She breathed out slowly, her lips pursed together, her breath making a shaky whistling sound. "Okay," she said. "All right."

After a minute, she looked up and smiled. "Are you ready to bake?"

That was why Grandma Sissy was down here—she wanted to show Odette and Rex how to bake their favorite cookies.

"Me first," said Rex.

Gary had laid out everything they'd need to make snickerdoodles and double chocolate chip cookies, the flour and the right number of eggs and baking soda and cubes of yellow butter. Grandma Sissy sat in her chair and directed them, but she wouldn't touch a thing. "You'll need to be able to do this yourselves, after I'm gone." She wouldn't even let Mom help Rex, other than pouring the liquids.

When he cracked an egg and got some on his fingers, Rex freaked out for a couple of minutes. He hated anything slimy on his hands. But Grandma Sissy told him, "It's just eggs—go wash your hands and buck up, little soldier," which Rex thought was funny. He double-washed his hands and went back to work.

Textures were just something that freaked Rex out. And snickerdoodles weren't cookies you could make without getting your hands dirty. Odette watched, amazed, as

Rex scooped a handful of cookie dough, rolling it into a ball, and then dipping it in a sugar-cinnamon mix before placing it on a cookie sheet.

"Well done, little soldier," Grandma Sissy said when his cookies were finished and in the oven. Then it was Odette's turn.

Mom and Dad took Rex out for a walk and left Odette alone with Grandma Sissy.

"Don't let my cookies burn," Rex told Odette.

Technically, Odette didn't even need Grandma Sissy there. She could just follow the recipe, written out in Grandma Sissy's loopy script on an index card. But she listened as Grandma Sissy walked her through the steps.

"Always use real butter," Grandma Sissy said. "Never margarine. And let it soften to room temperature on its own. Set it out at least an hour before you plan to bake. The cookies turn out better that way." She motioned for Odette to hand her a cube of butter, and she squeezed it a little. Underneath the wax paper, the butter dented in the shape of Grandma Sissy's thumb.

"Perfect," Grandma Sissy said as Odette unwrapped the cube and dropped it into the bowl. She shook in a cup of fine white sugar and turned on the mixer, creaming the butter and sugar together.

"Now," Grandma Sissy said, "the recipe says to add in the eggs and vanilla. But let me share a secret with you. Add the vanilla first, before the eggs. And then stop."

Odette measured out a teaspoonful of vanilla extract, smelling it before she tipped it into the bowl. She blended it into the sugar and butter mixture and then turned to Grandma Sissy. "Get two spoons," Grandma Sissy said.

Odette did, and Grandma Sissy told her, "Scrape out a little bit onto each spoon. Not a whole spoonful. That would throw off the recipe. Just a taste."

Then Grandma Sissy motioned for Odette to bring her a spoon. "This is my favorite thing in the world," she said, taking one of the spoons.

Odette tasted the mixture. Smooth butter, granular sugar, vanilla. That was all.

It was perfection.

Grandma Sissy smiled. "Baker's privilege," she said. "I think this is even yummier than the cookies."

Stitching and Loosening

I SHALL SEW IT on for you, my little man,' she said, though he was tall as herself, and she got out her sewing bag, and sewed the shadow on to Peter's foot."

Mom had found an old copy of *Peter Pan* on one of Grandma Sissy's bookshelves, and she was reading it aloud to Rex while he practiced jacks on the floor. Georgie, perched again on Grandma Sissy's lap, watched the bouncing ball with interest. At the table, Odette and Dad were playing solitaire together, a "contradiction in terms," he said, but much more fun than playing alone.

Mom read on: "'I daresay it will hurt a little,' she warned him.

"'Oh, I shan't cry,' said Peter, who was already of the opinion that he had never cried in his life. And he clenched his teeth and did not cry, and soon his shadow was behaving properly, though still a little creased."

Grandma Sissy opened her eyes. "That's a funny bit," she said. "About the shadow."

"I like that part," said Rex. "It's my favorite."

"Mine too," said Grandma Sissy. "It reminds me of me. Except instead of sewing my shadow on, I'm pulling at the threads that hold my soul to my body."

None of them knew what to say to that. Mom closed the book and reached over to hold Rex's hand. Dad mislaid a card in the game, and Odette didn't have the heart to point out his mistake.

Then Rex said, "Well, it's your soul, after all. Why shouldn't you untie it, if it's ready to go free?"

Grandma Sissy smiled. "Wisely spoken," she said, and then she closed her eyes.

The Last Thing

"HOW WILL IT work?" Odette asked her dad.

"How will what work?" Dad asked. But then he looked up, and Odette could tell that he knew what she meant. "Oh, honey," he said. "Do you really need to hear the details?"

Odette nodded.

Dad sighed. "Mom will open the capsules of medicine and pour out the powder into a glass of water. That's all. Once it dissolves, Grandma Sissy just has to drink it down."

"What does it taste like?"

"It's supposed to be pretty bitter," Dad said.

"And that will be the last thing she tastes? Ever? Something bitter?"

"I don't think the taste will bother her much, honey."

It wasn't fair. That someone as sweet as Grandma Sissy should die with a bitter taste in her mouth.

Star-Full Sky

I T WAS ABSURD, but in the middle of the night, Odette wanted the photo from Sacramento, the one of her and Mom as saloon girls. She woke suddenly, her wide eyes blind in the dark.

The room around her was full of sleep—Georgie tucked under the covers, in the crook of Odette's knees, Rex on the pulled-out trundle bed beneath her. Paul, too, was silent in his cage.

But Odette was awake. And somehow, she couldn't wait until morning to retrieve the picture. As quietly as she could, Odette freed herself from the blankets, tucking them firmly around Georgie. Maneuvering carefully around Rex's sleeping body, Odette managed to make it to the door without waking anybody. In the hallway, a finger of light glowed from the crack beneath the closed door to her parents' room; Grandma Sissy's doorway was dark.

Tiptoeing down the stairs and through the bakery, Odette focused only on being very, very quiet. She barely breathed. And before she opened the bakery's door to the street, she palmed the little bell that hung from the handle to silence it.

The concrete sidewalk was damp and cold beneath Odette's bare feet, and the air was seawater-salty with each breath. Above her, the satin sky glowed with starlight. So many stars, thousands of them, uncountably many. They shimmered up there—they vibrated. If each star were a wish, Odette thought, she could use them all.

Just down the street squatted the Coach. Odette hurried toward it, shivering in her nightgown, but as she reached for the silver door handle, she realized that it was probably locked and that she didn't have the key. Still, she pulled at the handle, just in case. The handle popped forward. The door swung open, and those two little metal steps slid out like an eager tongue to greet her.

It was almost too easy. Odette climbed the two steps and reached behind her to pull the door shut. When it clicked closed, Odette realized that she'd missed that sound, the tinny little noise of the latch catching. It sounded, in an odd and surprising way, like home felt.

"Liz?" came her dad's voice, from the back of the Coach. "Is that you?"

Odette squeaked, a high-pitched, scared sound. Her throat clenched tight.

"Odette?" Dad asked. He fumbled and swore, and switched on a light. Odette saw that he was in his pajamas, tucked into bed. He was sleeping there, in the Coach. Not upstairs, with Mom. And her throat clenched tighter, with sadness instead of fear, and her eyes stung with tears.

"Honey," Dad said.

"Do you sleep out here every night?" Odette asked, her voice thick with shame at finding this—her dad, sneaking out to sleep alone, and the look on his face now that she knew his secret.

"Oh, honey," he said.

"Are you and Mom going to get a divorce?"

There. She'd said it.

"Oh, honey," Dad said again. "No, of course not." Then, "I mean, I hope not. *We* hope not."

It was too much. Too much by far. Grandma Sissy, and moving so far from home, and the way Rex was, and this terrible thing with Mom and Dad. It wasn't fair, none of it was fair, none of it was even her *fault*.

"I just wanted to get my picture," Odette said. "But I can get it in the morning." And when she clicked closed the Coach's door, this time from the outside, it sounded not like home but rather like the end of something.

August Third

ON AUGUST THIRD, Grandma Sissy died.
She said that she preferred to think of it as "loosening her soul," and Odette tried to think about it that way too. She had said she would stay as long as she could, "until the pain was greater than the pleasure of living." Lately, she slept so much that sometimes it felt like she was already dead.

Odette still wasn't sure if she agreed with what Grandma Sissy had decided to do. Odette knew she was in pain. She saw her taking pain pills all the time, and she could barely remember seeing Grandma Sissy eating in days and days. But still. To take medicine on purpose like that. It scared Odette. It really, really did.

"Her decision" were words she heard a lot, from Mom, and Dad, and Bea and Gary, too. "So much pain." She heard that, too. "Support her. Love her."

Grandma Sissy didn't want anyone but Mom in the room when she drank the medicine, but after she drank it, Mom opened the door to let them come inside.

A small clear glass sat on the table next to Grandma Sissy's bed. There was a milky residue at the bottom.

"Darlings," Grandma Sissy said. Her voice was wobbly but she smiled at them. "Darling darlings."

Georgie jumped up onto the bed right beside her and curled into a little ball. Rex kissed her, and so did Dad, and Mom. It was Odette's turn then. She didn't know until the last moment if she'd have the nerve, but then she did, and after she kissed Grandma Sissy, she held out the spoon she'd prepared. Eyes half-closed already, Grandma Sissy opened her mouth. Odette placed the butter-sugar-vanilla mixture on her tongue. Grandma Sissy held it in her mouth for a moment before swallowing. Her eyes closed all the way, and she smiled. In a moment Grandma Sissy was asleep, and minutes later she wasn't breathing anymore.

Then Mom started crying really loudly, and Georgie whined. Dad picked up the dog and said, "She was a good woman. We were all lucky."

Even Rex was crying. Through his tears he said, "She doesn't look dead. Are you sure she's dead?"

Odette didn't agree. Grandma Sissy *did* look dead. Her soul had been loosened. She had loosened her very own soul.

Odette took Georgie from Dad and left the room. She sat down in Grandma Sissy's chair. As she sat, she smelled Grandma Sissy—her soap, her perfume. She closed her eyes and breathed.

Awakening

WHEN ODETTE WOKE, it was to a world without Grandma Sissy.

How, she wondered, could life go on after wonderful people leave it? Then Georgie licked Odette's nose, and dug her sharp little paws into Odette's chest, and wagged her tail. And life did indeed go on.

Odette walked Georgie around the village. It was raining, a soft misty rain as if some of the ocean had been caught in a wind current and was now drifting slowly back down.

The village felt quiet, shuttered, as if everyone was still in bed. Perhaps they were. If she hadn't needed to walk Georgie, Odette would have stayed in bed too. How much of life is that, she wondered — getting up because someone else needs you to, doing a task because it has to be done?

Walking suddenly didn't feel like a strong enough statement, so Odette began to jog, and then she ran. The dog ran too, keeping pace in spite of her short little legs. Georgie looked up at her as if to ask, *Is this good? Are we happy?* and Odette answered, "Good girl."

When finally Odette and Georgie circled back to the house, she saw that no one had come to open the bakery; the CLOSED sign stayed turned outward in the window.

Upstairs, the rooms were all quiet—her parents' room, the room she shared with Rex, and Grandma Sissy's room, most of all.

I Wish

GRANDMA SISSY LIKED to travel, didn't she?" Odette and Mom were in Grandma Sissy's room, flipping through old scrapbooks. Grandma Sissy was in barely any of the photos—she was behind the camera. The scrapbooks were full of pictures of buildings, labeled "Eiffel Tower," "New York Skyline," "Hardwick Hall," and page after page of houses. Big stately places. Funny little cottages. New houses. Old houses.

And there—unexpectedly, suddenly—there was a picture of their house. The red front door. The tipsy brick footpath. The shutters. The windows. Odette imagined she could see behind the door, behind the windows. The mud bench inside. The pink-ceilinged bedroom. Who knew what color the Waldmans had painted her room?

Mom's finger traced the roofline. "You miss it?"

Odette nodded. "Do you?"

"Sure I do," Mom said. She flipped away from the picture of their house, to a page full of thatched-roofed cottages. "Grandma Sissy always said houses were her favorite art form."

Odette thought about that. Houses as art. "Mine too," she decided. "I like the ones here on the island."

"Mm-hmm," said Mom. "They're cute, aren't they?"

"Yeah."

"You like it here?"

"It's pretty cool," Odette said. "I like the bakery. It's not the same, though, now."

Now that Grandma Sissy was gone. Odette did miss their house back home. But not nearly as much as she missed Grandma Sissy.

"It's not fair," she said, quietly.

"What's not fair? That we sold the house?"

"Yes," said Odette. "And that Grandma Sissy died. And about you and Dad. And Rex. The way he is. Everything."

Mom sat so still for so long that Odette felt sure she was mad. But when she finally spoke, she didn't sound mad. "It's not Rex's fault that he is the way he is," Mom said.

"It's not my fault either," Odette answered.

Mom looked up at last. She looked, long and deep, right into Odette's eyes. Odette didn't want to break the gaze, she didn't want to be the first to look away, but after a minute it just felt too intense to keep staring, so she let her gaze slip to Grandma Sissy's bedspread.

"It's not your fault, Odette. Of course it's not your fault."

Odette felt the tear tickle her cheek, watched as it splattered on the bedspread and sank in.

Then Mom reached out and put her arm over Odette's shoulder. Odette held herself stiff and unlovable, but Mom scooted her in closer, and closer, and finally Odette let herself go soft and limp. Mom pulled her onto her lap even though Odette was years too big to fit. Her breath was hot and moist in Odette's hair, her sweater scratchy against Odette's teary cheek, but Odette didn't pull away.

"I'm so sorry, Detters," Mom said. "I wish I had answers for you. I wish I could bring Grandma Sissy back. I wish I could promise that everything will be okay."

"I wish people lived forever," Odette muttered into Mom's sweater.

Mom nodded. Odette could feel it against the top of her head. "I wish they did too."

"I wish Rex didn't have furies," Odette said.

"I wish life was always fair," Mom said.

Odette dried her eyes. "Me too."

Mom kissed Odette's hair. She pulled away a little so she could look into Odette's eyes, and dried Odette's tears with her thumbs. "You know," Mom said, "Grandma Sissy liked to say that fair didn't mean even. Fair means everyone getting what they need, not everyone getting the same thing."

Odette didn't have anything to say to this, so she just shrugged.

Then Mom said, "What do *you* need, Detters?"

What did she need? "I don't know," she said. "I thought I needed to stay home. I thought I needed a big dog. I thought I needed a phone."

"Those all would have been nice," Mom said. "I can understand why you'd want those things."

"No one asked me about moving," Odette said. She forced the words around the hard ball in her throat. "No one asked me about the dog, or the phone, or any of it."

Mom's face twisted up funny. "Not everything can be a democracy, Detters. Sometimes grownups have to make decisions."

"Yeah," said Odette. "I guess. Sometimes. But not always."

She could tell Mom wanted to argue. Mom *hated* being wrong. She wasn't good at being wrong. But instead of arguing, Mom said, "Okay, Detters. I hear you. If we can take a vote, next time we will."

"Really?"

Mom nodded. "Really. But tell me . . . about Georgie. She's way better than a Labrador, right?"

"Yeah," Odette conceded. "I wouldn't trade her for a dozen Labs."

Bacon Training

HOW DO YOU get her to do that?" Rex asked from his perch on the steps of Grandma Sissy's bakery. Georgie was sitting balanced on her butt, her front legs in front of her chest like a little squirrel. Her black eyes followed Odette's hand as it traced a pattern—left, up, right, down, again and again.

"I trained her with bacon," Odette answered. Then, to Georgie, she said, "Come!," and the little dog trotted over for her reward, which Odette retrieved from a plastic bag in her pocket, a little scrap of crispy bacon.

"How'd you learn to do that?" Rex asked.

Odette shrugged. "Dogs like bacon."

Rex was quiet for a minute. Then he asked, "Do you think we could train Paul like that? To listen and wait and come on command?"

"That depends, I guess."

"On what?"

Odette smiled. "On how much Paul likes bacon."

"I'll go get him," Rex said, and he stood up and ran inside, the bakery's door jingling behind him.

For a minute, Odette felt annoyed. She'd come out to be here alone, and now Rex was going to make the whole afternoon about him. But on the other hand, he was her brother. And maybe it was kind of cool that he wanted her help.

She looked back at Georgie, who was waiting smart as could be, her eyes trained on Odette's hand. "Good girl," Odette said.

The bell sounded again. Still focused on Georgie, Odette asked, "Are you ready?"

"Always," said Dad. Odette looked up, surprised, and Georgie dashed forward to snatch the bit of bacon from her hand.

"Was she supposed to do that?" Dad asked, looking amused.

"She's a work in progress," Odette said.

"Aren't we all," Dad said. He leaned against the

handrail and watched Odette pull out another scrap of bacon, watched Georgie's eyes follow the bacon in Odette's hand—up, down, left, right.

"Up," said Odette to her dog, and Georgie leaned back on her heels, sitting up proud and tall, never taking her gaze off the bacon. "Good girl," Odette said, and tossed the treat to Georgie, who caught it neatly.

"She's a smart one," Dad said.

"Uh-huh," said Odette. Then she said, "I guess I never thanked you for getting her for me."

"Nope," said Dad with a smile. "You didn't. Not yet."

"Well," said Odette. "Thank you. Georgie is the perfect dog for me."

"You are welcome," Dad said. "And thank *you,* too."

"For what?"

"For being my kid," he answered. "You and Rex are the perfect kids for me."

Odette smiled, even though it was a goofy thing for him to say. She wanted to ask, *What about Mom? Is she perfect for you too?* But she didn't.

Her parents had been holding hands a lot. A few times Odette had listened outside their bedroom door to hear both of their voices, late at night. Once or twice she had even heard them laughing. Part of her wanted to make Dad promise that everything would be okay with him and Mom. Instead she said, "Watch this. I'm trying to teach Georgie how to walk on her hind legs."

Then Rex came out with Paul, who must have been sleeping, because his eyes were squinty and he kept yawning. "Okay," he said. "Here he is. Give him some bacon. Let's see if he likes it."

We Could

IT WAS THE day of Grandma Sissy's memorial, two weeks after she had died. They had held it as an open house at the bakery, and all of them—Mom, Dad, Odette, Rex, Bea, Gary, everyone—had baked for three days in preparation.

They made Grandma Sissy's favorites, cupcakes and individual chocolate cream pies, and they made her signature breads, mixed fruit popovers, bread pudding, and cookies, cookies, cookies.

They baked so that they would have enough to feed every resident of Eastsound Village and all of Grandma Sissy's friends from the mainland who would be coming to the memorial, and then they baked even more because it seemed like something Grandma Sissy would want them to do—to sift and roll and fold and pound and bake.

They baked and they served and they cleaned up after. Never had Odette seen the bakery so full. People kept coming up and introducing themselves — "You must be Sissy's granddaughter. You look just like her. You bake like her too!" and "Your grandmother was such a fine woman. Such a fine, grand woman." Gary sniffed and wiped his eyes with a blue gingham pocket square. Bea claimed that crying was for tragedies and this wasn't a tragedy, it was a blessing. Over and over everyone said how much they loved Grandma Sissy, and how they would help out any way they could.

Now, at last, the crowd had gone away and all that was left was flour caked under fingernails, stomachaches from too many sweets, and each other.

They flopped in Grandma Sissy's living room, Mom on the chair and Odette with Rex and Dad on the sofa. Rex wore Paul in his ferret pouch around his neck. It had turned out that Paul liked bacon quite a lot, and that he was amenable to learning tricks to earn it. He was, however, developing a tiny potbelly under his fur. Georgie, exhausted from cleaning up cookie scraps, lay at their feet. When after a long time of quiet Mom finally spoke,

Georgie's ears perked up into two little points and she tilted her head as if she was listening.

"We could stay," Mom said. Her voice was barely more than a whisper.

No one answered. The most important word in that sentence, Odette thought, wasn't "stay." It was "we." As in, all of them. Together.

"There are schools on the island," Mom went on. "And Grandma Sissy left the bakery to me. We could stay."

"Stay here?" said Rex, the first to respond. "On the island? We could run the bakery?"

Mom nodded.

Rex looked surprised, but Odette wasn't. It made sense: Mom was Grandma Sissy's only child.

"Would Gary still help? And Bea? Would they be our friends?" Rex asked.

"I think they already *are* our friends," Mom said, smiling. "But yes, they have offered to help out as long as necessary—teaching us about ordering and billing and more recipes."

"What about the Coach?" Odette asked.

Mom looked at Dad. His head lolled against the back of the couch and his feet rested on the coffee table. As the official dishwasher, he'd worked hard all day. "We'd sell it," he answered without opening his eyes.

We. He'd said "we" too.

Odette imagined what it might be like, to stay here on Orcas Island. She imagined riding her bike up Main Street with a group of kids. She pictured herself behind the counter of the bakery on the weekends. She imagined decorating a bedroom in Grandma Sissy's house, making it her own. Never climbing into the wretched Coach again. Not living on the road. No more wheels beneath her bed.

But if they stayed here, it wasn't as if everything would magically become the same as it used to be. Their problems wouldn't go away, not on their own.

"Could we buy kayaks with the money from the Coach?" Rex asked.

"Maybe," said Mom. And, to Odette, "But more than anything else, we want to hear from you. From both of you."

"*We* get to decide?" asked Rex. "Me and Odette?"

"We *all* get to decide," said Mom. She caught Odette's eye and smiled. "We'll take a vote. We know how rough this has been."

That was an understatement. Selling their home. Saying goodbye. Living in the cramped, ugly Coach. The tire blowout. Searching for Paul in the rain. The fight with Mieko. Losing the phone. Grandma Sissy dying. All of it had been terrible.

But.

"I don't know," Odette said, slowly.

Dad opened his eyes. His eyebrows rose to make crinkles in his forehead. "You don't want to stay?"

Part of her wanted to stay. Part of her wished they had never come in the first place. But if they hadn't, then they wouldn't have been here, with Grandma Sissy, at the end of her life. Witnessing her death had been terrible. But it had been better than *not* being there. Than *not* having kissed her goodbye.

Odette looked around at the pictures on the walls, the comfortably worn furniture, the wide, bright windows.

Outside and down the block waited the Coach. As tight and cramped as it was, it had kept the four of them — plus pets — warm and dry.

Far behind them, and long ago, was the house they had left behind.

"Grandma Sissy used to say that a beginning and an ending are two sides of the same door," Odette said.

"What the heck is that supposed to mean?" asked Rex.

"Maybe it means that on the other side of something sad is something happy," Dad said.

"Maybe it means that you can't see what's ahead of you if you're focused on what's behind you," Mom said.

Odette said, "I think it means that beginnings can't happen without endings. They're stuck together. They're connected."

"Well," Rex said, "she should have told us what she meant."

That made everybody laugh. Even Georgie barked sharp and loud like an exclamation point.

Right then, with doors ahead of them and behind them too, there they were. Together. And happy, even though there were plenty of good reasons not to be. That's life, as Grandma Sissy said. The good and the bad, all mixed up together.

They had come a long way from home. But Odette didn't feel homesick anymore.

Acknowledgments

FAR FROM FAIR, in its first drafts, was like a brain with two healthy hemispheres that lacked the connecting highway of the corpus callosum. It's due entirely to Adah Nuchi that the final version you hold in your hands feels like a whole brain, if it indeed does. I've compared Adah in the past to a jockey who knows where to drive me forward and when to reign me in; with this project, Adah was a surgeon and psychologist, helping me build bridges in the emotional landscape this story aims to illustrate. I am deeply grateful for her passionate, scalpel-sharp direction.

HMH has become the editorial home for my middle grade work that every writer hopes to find. I'm so very thankful for the support of Jeannette Larson, Betsy Groban, Mary Wilcox, Meredith Wilson, Lisa DiSarro, Helen Seachrist, Amy Carlisle, and Alison Miller, who have all touched the book in its various forms. And book designer Sharismar Rodriguez and illustrator Julie McLaughlin have given me back the text of my book in its perfect physical manifestation. Thank you.

As always, Rubin Pfeffer, thank you for being my partner and friend in the publishing world. I'm so grateful for you.

Most of all, I want to acknowledge Karen and Ted Negus and Rick and Clancey Arnold—my kids' grandparents—and my own grandmother, Frieda Kuczynski. In various ways, each of you has supported me, my family, and my writing, and none of my books could have been finished without you.

Sasha, Zak, and Mischa, my wonderful

siblings—thank you for being my friends as well as my family.

And, always, to Keith, Max, and Davis, who climbed with me into an ugly old RV and took the journey together that inspired this book. I love you.